Readers love
ALLISON CASSATTA

Patient Privilege

"The ultimate romantic in me really liked how the writer concluded
Erik and Angel's story. It was tactful, peaceful and romantic."
—Love Bytes

"This wasn't a love story per say, more of a story about two men that
had to find themselves before they found each other, the love they
found was just a bonus. I definitely recommend this read."
—MM Good Book Reviews

Teaching Professor Greyson

"This story is not all roses and sunshine. It is gritty…"
—Prism Book Allaince

We Found Love

2015 Rainbow Awards Honorable Mention

"Wow! What a beautifully written story this is… I was riveted from
beginning to end."
—The Blogger Girls

"I really enjoyed the concept, damaged guys are my weakness.
These two hit all the marks for me."
—Scattered Thoughts and Rogue Words

By ALLISON CASSATTA

With Tracey Michael: Beast
Dream 'til Monday
Kissing is Easy
Patient Privilege
Sins of the Heart
With Kade Boehme: Teaching Professor Grayson
With Remmy Duchene: This is Love
Three Little Words
With Kade Boehme: We Found Love

DEAR DIARY
Dear Diary
Pride
Relationships 101

SIN & SEDUCTION
Sin & Seduction
Lies & Seduction
The Final Seduction

Published by DREAMSPINNER PRESS
www.dreamspinnerpress.com

THREE Little WORDS

Allison Cassatta

Published by

DREAMSPINNER PRESS

5032 Capital Circle SW, Suite 2, PMB# 279, Tallahassee, FL 32305-7886 USA
www.dreamspinnerpress.com

Three Little Words

Cover Art
Cover content is for illustrative purposes only and any person depicted on the cover is a model.

ISBN: 978-1-63477-566-3
Digital ISBN: 978-1-63477-567-0
Library of Congress Control Number: 2016905996
Published August 2016
v. 2.0
First Edition published by Amber Quill Press, 2013.

Printed in the United States of America
∞
This paper meets the requirements of
ANSI/NISO Z39.48-1992 (Permanence of Paper).

This book is dedicated to the people who read my work, who continuously support me and encourage me.

ACKNOWLEDGMENTS

ALSO, I would like to thank Lynne Conn, Kristie Rifkin, and Jessica Murchie for beta-reading, as well as the fine staff at Dreamspinner Press for always taking such great care of my babies and giving them a good home.

CHAPTER ONE

"I THOUGHT you were picking me up from the airport," Matt yelled from the front door, dragging a suitcase and duffel bag behind him. His plane had landed almost two hours ago, and he hadn't heard a damn word from Brandon. Matt's boyfriend wasn't usually the type to disappoint.

He dropped his suitcase by the door and shrugged out of his leather jacket, then hung it on the metal coat rack in the foyer. The house was quiet, too quiet, but Brandon had to be home, because their car was in the driveway, parked right next to Matt's motorcycle. Where it was supposed to be. Matt frowned as he peered through the arched opening, scouring the living room for some sign of life.

The room was dark, the air cool. Everything appeared as clean and neat as usual. Brandon liked to play homemaker to Matt's handyman. He liked to keep an orderly house, the kind of home Matt had grown up in and always loved. Matt liked the warm, earthy tones Brandon had chosen when they bought the house. He loved the way Brandon's minimalist style still made the place cozy. It was perfect.

Dinner normally waited on the kitchen table when Matt got home from work, and it was never some frozen, prefabbed meal. Brandon took the time to make everything delicious and never skimped when it came to cuisine. He always took care of everything for Matt and kept the laundry done and everything spotless. Hell, no one would've even known they had a dog, because the scent of animal didn't exist. All he could smell was the sandalwood air freshener Brandon seemed to love so much.

After being gone for three weeks, he expected Brandon to be there, eagerly waiting for his return with open arms. That damn sure didn't appear to be the case.

"Brandon?" he called out. "Zeus?"

Matt raked his fingers through his messy brown hair, frowning harder as he headed toward the kitchen.

1

Again, the room was dark—dark granite countertops bare and clean. It didn't look like Brandon had even considered cooking a welcome-home meal. Brandon would've normally gone all out and made some elaborate dinner to celebrate Matt's return. Then they would've spent the night making up for the weeks they'd been apart. From the looks of it, Brandon had forgotten Matt was even coming home.

From the bay window overlooking their immaculate backyard, just beyond the breakfast nook that had originally sold them on the house, he spotted Zeus—the honey-brown pit bull puppy he'd rescued from the animal shelter by accident—lying on the patio beneath the canopy of a giant old Japanese maple tree. The pup looked content, food and water bowls still full. The way Zeus devoured whatever was put down in front of his face meant someone had recently tended to him.

So where the hell was Brandon?

With new urgency in his step and the new speed of his pulse, Matt quickly headed toward the back of the house, where they both had offices and a bedroom to share. He checked Brandon's office first, hoping he would find Brandon pounding away at a new novel. He wasn't there. Then Matt checked his man cave, even though Brandon rarely darkened its doors. He just had to be sure. Nothing. The bedroom was just as dark and empty too. Brandon wasn't there.

The moment Matt reached into his jeans pocket for his cell phone to give Brandon a call, he spotted a yellow piece of paper with black writing on the edge of the dresser. Brandon would've never left anything like that just lying around. It would've driven him crazy. And the closer Matt got to the dresser, the more he could make out what had been written on the page—a letter, with Brandon's signature.

His heart sank in his chest and collided with his stomach. Sure, it could've been a simple "ran to the grocery, be back later," but Matt knew better. Brandon wouldn't have abandoned him at the damn airport for a trip to the grocery store, or anything else, for that matter. No, this wasn't going to be one of *those* notes.

Taking a deep breath, Matt reached for the yellow page. He closed his eyes and exhaled slowly as he silently encouraged himself to man up and read the damn letter. In his heart, he already knew what it said. Right before he'd left for work three weeks ago, they'd gotten into a huge fight about all of his traveling. Matt tried like hell to convince Brandon that he wouldn't go if he could make as much money staying home. Unfortunately, he couldn't. Unfortunately, he wanted to give Brandon everything he wanted or needed, and Brandon didn't have cheap tastes.

He flipped the page over, opened his eyes, and stared down at the writing. At first, he couldn't focus on the words, like his brain refused to comprehend Brandon's messy scribble. He blinked a few times, then brought the page closer to his face.

> *Matt,*
> *I love you, but this isn't working anymore. I want someone who is going to be there when I need them. I know you have to work, and maybe I'm being selfish, but this is what I need. I love you. I'll always love you, but I need more.*
> *Brandon*

The page fell from Matt's hand and flittered to the floor. It landed at the tips of his black steel-toed boots. He couldn't sit down and couldn't move from that spot despite his suddenly quivering legs. His chest ached, and his eyes burned, but he didn't cry. Matt wouldn't cry, and that was yet another item on the list of imperfections Brandon had so eloquently pointed out during their last screaming match.

How dare Brandon break up with him on a piece of legal paper? Who the hell did that?

Who did Brandon think he was?

Did Matt not deserve better?

Holy shit.

Suddenly, the backs of his knees hit the edge of the bed the two of them had been sharing for the last five years. Matt wasn't even aware of stumbling back toward it. He just found himself sitting without making a conscious choice to do so.

He rubbed his sweaty palms over his tattered, faded jeans and hung his head. As much as he'd been looking forward to being in his own bed again, there was no way in hell he could sleep without Brandon beside him. Brandon's light snoring in his ear had become a lullaby over the years, and Brandon's warmth against his chest as Matt spooned his lover's back was better than any blanket.

Now it was gone.

Scrubbing his meaty, work-calloused hands against his face, he sighed and fell back on the bed. His bags were still at the front door, and Zeus was still locked up in the backyard, but Matt didn't have the wherewithal to deal with any of it right now. Frankly, he wished he could rewind time and go back to the moment he began losing Brandon, the moment they stopped being best friends and started feeling more like acquaintances.

"Shit, I knew this was coming," Matt muttered in realization.

Yes, he had been aware of their problems, their disconnection. He'd seen something extraordinarily different in Brandon's otherwise-light, shimmering hazel eyes during that last explosive fight. There was a foreboding darkness, and before Matt had left for his three-week stint in New Orleans, he'd felt Brandon's distance.

The phone in his pocket started to ring, and Matt debated ignoring it. There wasn't really anyone he needed or wanted to talk to right now—Brandon included. But the longer he lay there and let it ring, the more pissed off he became, so angry in fact, he thought he might grind his teeth down to nothing. The whole time, he hadn't realized he was clenching his jaw so tightly.

He dipped his hand into his denim pocket and wrapped his fingers around the phone, lifted it to his face, and stared blankly at the screen. It was his mother, more than likely calling to make sure he'd made it home safely.

Great.

Now wasn't a good time to talk to her. He could try to hide behind carefully chosen words and a flat tone of voice, but his mother was too intuitive for her own good. She could read him better than

4

anyone. But if he didn't answer, she would worry, maybe even come looking for him.

Time to face the music.

"Hello?" he answered with a sigh.

"You sound exhausted," she said, voice dainty and demure. She always sounded so soft and elegant… until someone pissed her off. "Was your flight that bad, honey?"

"No, ma'am," he softly responded. "I sat in the airport for two hours waiting for Brandon before finally calling a cab. When I got home, no one was here and Zeus was locked up in the backyard."

"That doesn't sound like Brandon. Is everything okay?"

Matt sat up on the bed and looked down at the curling yellow paper lying on the floor, at the angry scribbles and the way Brandon had claimed he still loved him. He pressed his elbow to his knee and rested his forehead on his palm. Closing his eyes, he exhaled slowly.

"Matty?" his mom said. The inquisitive tone of her voice, the *I-know-something's-up* lilt, triggered that sensation all sons got when their mothers knew they were hiding something. "What happened, Matty?"

"He's gone, Mom," he said, voice low.

"Gone where?"

"I don't know. Gone."

"What happened?"

"He left me a letter that said he needed to go." Matt shrugged, even though his mom couldn't see him. "Said things weren't working and he needed more, but he still loves me."

"Baloney!" And there was her angry voice. "How is he going to break up with you on a damn letter and tell you he loves you?"

"I don't know, Mom."

"That's just not right."

"I know."

"Well, what are you going to do?"

"I don't know."

"What do you mean you don't know?"

"I found the letter ten minutes before you called. I haven't brought Zeus in. I haven't unpacked my bags. Honestly, I haven't thought about anything except for the fact that I'm alone now." Matt took another deep breath. He could feel his temper flaring, and God help him, if he got snippy with his momma over this mess, she wouldn't let him forget it.

"Sorry," he finally said. "I'm just tired, and I can't deal with this crap right now."

"Why don't you rest, then call me when you're feeling up to it? We'll figure all this mess out."

"Thanks. I love you, Mom."

"I love you too, son. Now, get some sleep."

"I will."

Standing from the bed, he ended the call and tossed the phone onto his dresser, then headed out of his room, back down the hall, and into the kitchen. Zeus already sat on his haunches at the back door, staring up at the window as if he felt his master's presence before Matt had even entered the room. He opened the door, and the fifty-pound pit bull puppy all but leapt into his arms. At least someone was happy to see him. At least someone greeted him with kisses. Zeus wagged his tail with excitement as he licked at Matt's face. Matt hugged the puppy tight against him, and in that moment, he finally broke down.

Tears fell hard and fast, rolling down his cheeks and dripping onto the pup's soft brown coat. Zeus whimpered and nudged his snout at his master's cheek. The dog knew something was amiss.

"What am I going to do?" Matt cried, brushing his hand up and down Zeus's fur. "I can't stay here without him."

The house just didn't feel right without Brandon in it. Hell, the world didn't feel right without him. Now, Matt just wanted to escape it all. Everything in the house reminded him of what he'd lost, and for what? Because he wanted to do the best he could for the person who meant the most to him?

CHAPTER TWO

TWO WEEKS and more than twenty phone calls later—one telling Brandon he could have the car Matt had bought him—and Matt was no closer to closure than he had been when he'd read that letter from the dresser. The pain remained. The disappointment in himself, in Brandon, in the both of them together, held strong. The anger continued to rage. And Matt began to believe it would never end.

He sat on the kitchen counter with a cold beer in his hand, absently picking at the edge of the label as he stared at a stack of boxes by the bay window of the breakfast nook they'd once loved so much. Zeus curled beneath his feet.

Everything Matt and Brandon had picked out for their house was packed in those boxes, every memory—good or bad—every gift Brandon had given him over the years, carefully cradled in Bubble Wrap. Those sad brown boxes were a testament to how horribly off track his life had gone. And to think, he'd planned to ask Brandon to marry him. Who knew things could go so wrong?

"I think I got it all," Luke said as he leaned against the arched opening leading into the kitchen. He swiped the last dishtowel from the counter beside him and scrubbed his dirty hands.

Matt looked up at his best friend of over twenty years and gave him a sad smile. "Thanks, bro."

"Hey, you did it for me when I moved away to become a fireman. It's the least I could do."

That had been about seven years ago, way before Matt met Brandon, back when Matt still wanted to be madly in love with his best friend. Matt never confessed and never would. Hell, he didn't even know if Luke was gay or straight. Luke never seemed too interested in dating—not a guy or a girl. He'd always focused on sports and working out. He had dreams he chased, and none of them ever included dating.

Sexuality was easy not to talk about. Sexuality was nonexistent in their world. Or that's what Matt always told himself.

Sometimes, on that rare occasion when he thought about growing up with Luke, Matt wondered if Luke ever knew how he felt, if it ever came out in a look or in something he'd said. Luke never asked, and Matt would never dare to talk about it. Not even now, after finding himself unexpectedly available. He'd worked hard to push those feelings aside when it seemed like the two of them would never be anything more than friends. Some subjects didn't need discussion. Ever.

The sunlight pouring in through the bare bay windows made the tan skin of Luke's naked muscled chest look almost bronze. It made his blond hair look a rich shade of gold. His blue eyes even seemed to sparkle as he stared right at Matt's face.

"Dude, you gotta snap out of this. You're killin' me," Luke said.

"Sorry, man. I'm trying. I just—" Matt shook his head as he hopped down from the counter, careful not to step on Zeus. "—can't believe he did this to me. I mean, fuck, I gave him everything he ever wanted."

"Yeah, and he's a damn fool to let someone like you go."

"Maybe." Matt shrugged.

"Do you need anything else from me?"

"Nah. Mom hired movers to come pick this shit up and take it to storage. She's keeping Zeus for me too."

"I thought your mom didn't have a yard or anything."

"Not at the condo she doesn't, but what else am I going to do with him?"

"Let me take him home. I have a huge yard. Plenty of running space."

Zeus popped up from the floor as if he knew they were talking about him. Tail wagging like crazy, he brushed his head against Matt's leg. Matt leaned down and began scratching the spot behind his ear. "You'd do that for me?" Matt asked, still looking down at his furry best friend.

"Hell yeah!"

"Man, I appreciate it. Zeus would be a hell of a lot happier with you. He knows you better than Mom, and you can play with him. She can't. She's just too old and not in any shape to be chasing around a puppy."

"You coming back for him?"

"Probably. When I get settled in… somewhere. I'll be on Mark's boat for a little while. We're taking off out of New England next week. I don't know what I'm gonna do after that. Might stay up there for a few months, see what happens."

"A few months with your brother? How are you gonna survive?"

"Who knows?" Matt said with a hint of laughter.

The conversation came to a dead halt. With a sigh, Matt stood, but Zeus didn't leave his side. He tried not to stare as Luke crossed the length of the galley kitchen. He tried like hell not to watch the flex of his best friend's muscles as Luke reached in the fridge and grabbed a bottle of beer.

"Hand me one too," Matt said.

And when Luke rose up from the fridge, he was face-to-face with Matt, and goddammit if Matt didn't want to pull him into a kiss. No, he wasn't over Brandon already, but he'd had this *thing* for Luke for half a lifetime and right now, he just wanted… someone, someone who wouldn't run out on him and leave him heartbroken. Luke would never do that. Even if he didn't have the same feelings, he'd never do anything to hurt Matt.

Luke pressed the cold, brown bottle to Matt's hand. Their eyes locked, and no matter how badly Matt wanted to, he couldn't force himself to look away. He took a breath and swallowed so hard he could hear the loud sound of his throat muscles tightening.

"You okay?" Luke asked.

"No. I'm not. I'm not okay at all."

The air surrounding them suddenly became thick and hard to breathe. Something in Luke's stare changed, though Matt couldn't really describe it. His eyes softened, darkened even, like maybe he had something he needed to get off his chest too, but maybe he was too afraid. Matt tensed his jaw and narrowed his eyes.

"What?" he asked in a bitter rush, because he couldn't stand the way Luke stared at him.

"I don't like seeing you this way, man. It's freaking me out."

"Why?"

"Because you're not this guy, Matt. You're… fun. You're lighthearted and always smiling. This shit ain't you, man."

"I'm trying. I gotta get out of this place. Everywhere I look, I see him. I don't want to see him anymore."

"I know," Luke said softly as he laid his hand on Matt's shoulder. The warmth of his palm felt like heaven on Matt's sweaty skin, even with the heat radiating from his pores. It was the kind of sincere, caring touch Matt needed.

He let out the breath he'd been holding and looked down, catching a glimpse of Luke's toned chest as he averted his eyes. If he kept looking at Luke, Matt would end up throwing caution to the wind and planting his lips against his best friend's mouth. He couldn't do that. He'd already lost one person he cared about. He couldn't lose another.

A strong, moist hand wrapped around his chin and lifted his head, forcing him to look at Luke again. That dark, weighty feeling returned to Luke's beautiful blue eyes. His stare made Matt's heart beat faster, then slower. And before Matt even had a chance to blink, Luke's lips landed on his.

At first he didn't know how to react. He didn't know what to think. His best friend of over twenty years—a man he'd assumed to be straight, a man he'd wanted to kiss the moment he laid eyes on him all those years ago—now had him in a lip lock, and for some stupid reason, Matt's brain shut down. He didn't know what the hell to think and couldn't make himself react.

"Sorry," Luke said in a breathless rush as he pulled away from the kiss.

Jesus Christ, Matt didn't want the kiss to end, and he damn sure didn't want Luke to apologize for giving him something he'd wanted for such a long time. But what else could Luke think? Matt had tensed on him. Matt hadn't kissed him back.

Matt had acted like a fool.

"I didn't… I mean, I thought—"

Luke's stammering came to an abrupt halt the moment Matt pulled him closer and clamped his lips over Luke's mouth. Luke closed his eyes first, and Matt immediately followed. He ran his hands around Luke's slender waist and pulled him into a hug as he pressed his tongue through the slight part of Luke's lips.

Their tongues twisted as their mouths caressed. Matt suddenly felt and heard the rush of his pulse as it pounded in his temples. He felt light as a feather, like floating through the cosmos, and it was the best he'd felt in over two weeks.

He moaned as their mouths opened and closed, kissing and caressing. He licked at the roof of Luke's mouth, tasting the hoppy beer they'd both been drinking. He felt the soft moistness of Luke's tongue exploring every dark corner. Then he felt Luke's arms encircle his waist, and Matt didn't want to let go.

The kiss deepened, became more passionate than Matt could've ever dreamed. It was the kind of kiss that would've led to ripping their clothes off, if they'd had more than just their jeans on in the first place. The kind of kiss that led to sex against the kitchen counter, that led to awkward postcoital moments between two friends who should never have sex. The kind of kiss that ended perfect friendships—and the moment that thought entered Matt's mind, he pulled away.

It took a few tries before Matt could make his eyes open, and when they finally did, his stare landed on Luke's swollen, red lips. Luke looked up at him. A frown curled his handsome, rugged features.

"Why did you stop?" Luke asked as he dropped his arms from Matt's waist.

"Because, this doesn't need to go any further."

"Why? Because you're leaving? You could always stay."

"No," Matt said, shaking his head as he put a bit of safe distance between them. "This doesn't need to happen. Not right now."

"What is 'this'? What did you think we were doing?"

"I know where kisses like that lead, and I... you—"

"Stop." Luke pressed his thick palm to the air. He licked his lips, then grabbed his beer. "You don't have to explain. It's not the right time."

"Luke—"

11

"No. Don't. Please." Luke downed half his beer, then set the nearly empty bottle on the counter. It dripped with condensation, just like his voice dripped with hurt. "You go do your thing. Do whatever healing you need to do. I'll keep your dog for you, and when you're ready, we'll talk about this, okay?"

"Yeah. Sure."

Reaching out, Luke held his arms open wide for Matt. At first, Matt couldn't bring himself to budge, but the look in Luke's steely blue eyes begged for that embrace, and Matt couldn't keep denying how badly he wanted to hold Luke in his arms again.

He took those few, careful steps, closing the space once again. They wrapped their arms around each other, and Luke kissed Matt's cheek, right where the edge of his jawbone met the lobe of his ear. Luke whispered, "You do what you need to do. I'll always be here."

Then Luke pulled away from the hug, turned toward Zeus, and patted his leg. "C'mon, boy. We gotta go," he said.

The dog swung his head back toward Matt and whimpered.

"Go on now," Matt mumbled, tears tightening his throat. He didn't want to see his two best friends in the whole wide world go, but he didn't have a choice. If he was going to heal his heart and head, he had to do this. He had to get out of that house and leave that life behind.

He watched Luke and Zeus leave, and dammit if he didn't want to drop to his knees and sob like a baby. Nothing in the world—not even Brandon's breaking up with some stupid Dear John letter—hurt like watching them walk away. But with the two of them gone, leaving that place suddenly became so much easier.

After waiting to hear the rumble of Luke's huge truck roar, then fade, Matt grabbed his leather jacket and stepped into his steel-toed boots. He walked out the door, then locked everything up tight behind him. He took one last look at the brick-and-mortar representation of what his life had become in five years, let out a sigh, then went straight to his Harley.

CHAPTER THREE

HEADING OUT of Memphis on 40 East toward Roanoke, Virginia, left a hell of a lot to be desired. Sure, the countryside was beautiful and all, but it was boring. Lonely and boring. Counting all the big rigs kept Matt entertained for a little while. Imagining what world lay behind the miles and miles of trees kept his mind off darker days. But no matter how hard he tried, his brain knew where it wanted to be. His heart knew what route it wanted to follow.

Zeus and Luke had looked so damn sad as they left him behind. Hell, he even thought about Brandon and how all of this mess could've been avoided had Brandon been man enough to talk things out with him. No, Brandon chose to be a coward, and his cowardice completely disrupted everyone's lives.

His ass had started to hurt two hours ago, and his eyelids were getting heavy. He'd been on the road for close to ten hours—stopping only for a smoke and a piss. Portsmouth, New Hampshire, was another twelve hours away, but Matt needed a break.

The roar of his V-twin engine purred to a low rumble as he pulled down the off-ramp. Matt chose the first travel center he saw and parked close to the front entrance. He stood from his bike and pulled a pack of Camels out of his jacket pocket. He'd quit smoking right after he and Brandon hooked up because Brandon thought it a disgusting habit. It was, but the nicotine high seemed to settle his nerves better than anything right now.

As he paced a short line up and down the front of the store, he rolled the butt of his cigarette between his thumb and forefinger and stared down at the bright orange cherry burning the smoke down to ashes. He was half-disgusted with himself for picking the habit back up again, and half-amused that he even cared.

"Hey there, cutie pie," a feminine voice said from behind him. "Nice bike."

He turned around, and what he found was a trampy, spandex-dress-clad hooker with stilettos and the worst fried blonde hair he'd ever seen. Matt snorted and flicked his cigarette out onto the driveway to join the other dead butts.

"I'm not interested," he said flatly as he stalked by her and headed for the door.

"C'mon, baby. Gimme a ride on your…. Big. Red. Bike."

The way she accented the last three words would've been comical if she hadn't been so tragic. Hell, if he hadn't been so tired, he might've casually chatted it up with her despite his not being interested in anything she had to offer. As it was, he just wanted to find a place to crash for a bit before hitting the road again, and he damn sure wasn't going to ask the hooker where he could find a hotel room, even though she probably knew better than anyone he could've asked.

Matt pushed through the glass doors and into the shop. A couple of old truckers stood by the coffee pots, arguing over politics and the state of the union. The woman behind the counter looked like she'd been on the rough side of life for a while and was either praying for the end of her shift or praying for death, maybe even a bit of both.

"Is there a hotel close by?" Matt asked.

The woman shrugged, and one of the truckers whipped his head around.

"Sure is," the burly old man said. "'Bout thirty miles east, right off forty. You'll see the sign from the interstate."

"Thanks, man," Matt said before heading over to the case of sodas to grab himself a bottle of root beer.

He paid the woman, who barely gave him a smile as she handed him his change. When he returned to his bike, he found the hooker climbing up into a big rig. He wondered what happened to the people who were supposed to care enough about her to keep her from doing something so careless. Did she have parents who cared? Was she a scorned lover like him? Or was selling her body the only means she had to get by?

14

Shaking his head, he tucked the root beer into one of the saddlebags, climbed onto his bike, and cranked his baby, waiting for her motor to idle down to a low rumble. His ass wasn't quite ready for all the vibrating again, but he didn't care. His ass could deal. Matt needed a bed for the night. He needed a place to rest and re-collect himself so he could finish making the trek up to New Hampshire where he would meet his brother, then hopefully get on with his life.

Matt hit the highway again, cruising along at five over the speed limit. Semis roared by. Cars passed him like he was sitting still. Then the rain came. Hard, pounding torrents of cool rain. It rolled off his jacket and off his helmet but soaked straight through his jeans, leaving a cold chill that seemed to radiate through to his bones. As if things couldn't get any worse....

He pulled up to the front door of the motel—not a hotel like the trucker had promised, not that the older man probably knew there was a difference—parked his Harley, and pulled off his helmet. He almost hated trudging his soaked ass though the doors, but he didn't have any other choice, and this place wasn't classy enough for anyone to give him a second look.

"Can I help ya, darlin'?" the gray-haired woman behind the counter called across the room, even before the automatic doors had a chance to close behind him.

"Need a room for the night."

"You sure do, don't ya? C'mon up here. Let's get ya signed in so ya can get outta them wet clothes."

Matt's boots sloshed with every step he took. It felt like stomping through mud. His wet socks and the waterlogged soles squished under his feet. It was probably one of the most uncomfortable things Matt had ever felt... well, save for the way his jeans and his boxer briefs were pinching his balls now. He reached in his back pocket and slapped his soggy wallet down on the counter, then carefully fished through it until he found his credit card.

"Damn, darlin', didn't ya watch the weather 'fore headin' out on a motorcycle? There's a tropical storm rollin' up from the Gulf."

"No," he said quietly. "The car belongs to my ex. I sold mine to get the bike. Didn't think we'd be breaking up before I could buy a new one."

"Some women never know what a good thing they got, huh?"

"Yeah," Matt snorted, without bothering to correct her. He could let her keep her comforting assumptions as long as he could get a room for the night.

"Okay, hon, you're gonna be in room one-twelve. Just go back out that door, and it'll be the sixth room. All the even numbers are on the front. Odd on the back, 'kay?"

"Got it."

"I gotta charge ya now. How many nights ya plan on stayin'?"

"Just one. I need to get back on the road first thing in the morning."

She took his credit card as she hoisted her rotund body from the well-worn desk chair she'd been sitting on, grunting as she made her way back toward what Matt assumed to be the credit card machine. She had an unmistakable hobble to her gait and definite bow to her spine, as if the weight she carried was doing a number on her old bones. But Matt wouldn't judge. Some people couldn't help it. His dad couldn't, and that's what ultimately led to his death.

"Alrighty, darlin', gotcha all set up." She handed him his credit card, and she sank back down on her trusty throne. He could tell by the rise and fall of her ample breasts her breathing was labored, and frankly, he felt a bit guilty for putting her through the stress. She smiled up at him and handed him the key to his room—not a card like all the nice hotels had, but an actual key with a hard, red, plastic keychain dangling from the end of it. "Enjoy your stay."

"Thank you."

The rain hadn't let up at all; in fact, it seemed to be coming down a bit harder now. Thank God he hadn't dried off at all, otherwise he might be a little put-off by having to go back into the thunderstorm.

Matt pulled his bike into the parking spot just outside room one-twelve. He parked in the dead center, killed the motor, and locked his baby up before darting to the door. The overhang did nothing for the rain being blown in by the southern winds, not that it mattered. He couldn't get much wetter than he already was, and the way he saw it, he might as well get used to it since he was about to take a job on a lobster boat.

The first thing he noticed was the obvious brown No Smoking sign on the door. Before the breakup, it wouldn't have bothered him. Now, he found himself more than annoyed that he couldn't kick back in nothing but his dry underwear and light up a smoke in the comfort of his cheap motel room.

He slipped the key in the door, fought to get it open, and he pushed with so much effort when the door finally freed itself of the jamb, it spilled him into a dark, dingy room.

The place was something straight out of a horror movie. The brown carpet looked like it had seen better days... back in the seventies. The comforter on the bed looked like it had been pulled from a dollar-store clearance rack. The television was one of those huge, bulky tube TVs people had been replacing with sleek flat-panel LCDs for years now, and dear God, the painting on the wall had to be one of those tacky inspirational prints.

Hell. Pure hell.

Matt wasn't a snob, but he had certain expectations of comfort, and that room did *not* fit the bill. He had to silently remind himself he wasn't on vacation, and he had to ignore the bad just so he could *try* to get some rest.

He shimmied his duffel bag straps off his shoulders, shrugged out of his leather jacket, which hit the floor with a thud, then came the boots. *Thump. Thump.* He then peeled away his wet jeans, underwear, and socks.

Standing in the middle of the room, completely naked and somehow still wet, he thought about how he'd left Memphis and who he left behind. He probably needed to call his mother and let her know he was still alive. Then there was Luke, who'd taken his pup home for a little TLC.

As if the powers that be had been listening in on his silent debating, the phone in his jacket pocket started to ring—a tacky '80s power ballad he'd fallen in love with back in elementary school, one that actually stuck with him for God only knew what reason. Maybe because it was a song that reminded him of hanging out with Luke. It was the reason the two of them had become friends in the first place. They'd actually spent hours debating the talent of the band and the greatness of their music.

The moment he looked down at the caller ID and saw the name on the screen, he sighed. "Luke." They hadn't spoken since the unexpected kiss, and he knew this conversation would be nothing less than awkward, even if the kiss didn't come up.

"Hey," he said into the phone's tiny mic hole.

"Hey, um, I just, uh…." There was an unmistakable air of caution in Luke's voice. "Where are you?"

"Virginia somewhere. Had to pull off for the night. The rain came down hard, and I just couldn't keep going."

"Good thing you pulled off."

"Yeah. How's Zeus doing?"

"He's fine. He knows something's up, though."

"Give it a night. He'll calm down."

"Yeah." There was a long pause. Matt could hear Luke's heavy breathing on the other end. Obviously Luke needed to talk, and it damn sure wasn't about the dog. "You got a minute?" Luke finally asked.

"Sure."

"About that kiss…."

And there they went, stepping off into the murky territory of their twenty-year relationship.

CHAPTER FOUR

BRUSHING HIS hand over his rain-soaked hair, Matt sank down on the mattress and pulled the scratchy comforter over his naked body. The chill had yet to leave his bones, and for this conversation, he wanted to be as comfortable as possible because he had a feeling this one wasn't going to end too soon.

"What about it?" Matt finally asked, training his eyes on the white popcorn pattern on the ceiling above his head. "You regretting it now?"

"I didn't say that," Luke blurted.

Matt heard him grunt, as if he'd stood from the couch or the bed or something. The years Luke had spent fighting fires had taken a toll on his body. Matt knew the cost of being a hero from the nights he'd spent by Luke's bed every time he ended up in the hospital after being hurt on the job, most of the accidents caused by Luke's clumsiness or his hurry. The guy had zero fear in the face of danger, and that alone made him a risk, but add to that the way Luke hurried through everything he did, and the guy was a walking disaster.

"Then what is there to talk about?" Matt asked.

"Did you um…. How did you…?"

"Did it turn me on?"

"Well, yeah and no. I sort of hoped…."

"Jesus, Luke, spit it out, man."

"I don't know what I want to say here. You're gone, and me kissing you isn't going to bring you back, is it?"

"No."

"Then why did you kiss me back?"

It was now Matt's turn to stand up and start pacing. His cold, damp jewels stuck to his inner thigh as he rolled out of the bed. The pain made him wince, and he immediately reached down to readjust.

"You really wanna know?"

19

"I asked, didn't I?"

"Because I've loved you almost as long as I've known you. I gave up about six years ago. Then I met Brandon, and everything was going good. I thought I could finally move on from you, and I had, until you kissed me. Then all those feelings started coming back."

"So why leave?"

"Because… I need to clear my head. I need to make sure I can get over Brandon. I was planning to marry him, for God's sake. We created a life together, and I honestly thought I would grow old with him. Do you know what it's like to realize the biggest, most important part of your life was a lie?"

"I can relate, Matt. My entire life has been a lie. I've been pretending to be someone else because I was afraid of accepting something I never believed could be true."

"And now? Am I supposed to be your experiment?"

"What the hell does that mean?" Luke all but growled.

"Am I the guy you're going to use to prove to yourself you can be in that kind of relationship? Am I the guy you want to come out of the closet with, or am I the waters you're gonna dip your toes in just to see how it feels to be gay?"

"That's a shitty thing to say, Matt. I'm being honest with you. I'm trying to tell you how I feel, and you're gonna go and say some shit like that to me? You can go to hell."

"Luke—"

"No. Don't. I was obviously very wrong for kissing you. It won't happen again."

"Luke, listen."

"There's nothing more to say."

And with that, the line went dead. Matt whispered, "I love you." But Luke wouldn't be lucky enough to hear those three little words, and by God, he sure as hell wouldn't be saying them again. Not anytime soon. Possibly not ever again.

He pitched his phone onto the center of the sagging bed and lay back with his legs hanging over the edge, stare fixed on the dizzying popcorn mess on the ceiling. Matt damn well knew he could go back to Memphis and tell Luke how he felt, and everything would probably be okay. In fact, things probably would be better than okay, but he feared that if he got involved with Luke right now, he would end up comparing the love of his life to the love of his adulthood. He would count the days until Luke decided to walk out on him just like Brandon did, because they all seemed to walk out on him. Luke did it, just because he wanted to play hero. What's his name—the guy he hooked up with when Matt was *trying* to be all scholarly—did it too, left him for some rich frat boy. And the list went on.

Matt just wasn't ready for that kind of heartache. He might've appeared cold and distant, but his heart was as big as the heavens, and though no one really saw it, Matt had a romantic side. He reserved that side for people who deserved it, men like Brandon—the one he wanted to marry, the one who broke up with him using a stupid damn Dear John letter.

Shit.

He lifted up from the edge of the bed and padded over to the duffel bag that had enough clothes to get him to New Hampshire, a few toiletries, and a wooden box he'd made in his shop class back in high school. It held every important keepsake Matt owned, which really wasn't much considering the long, somewhat meaningful relationships he'd had in his life.

With the box between his meaty hands, he backed away from the bag, and when the backs of his knees hit the edge of the bed, he sat back down. His stare remained fixed on the honey-colored pine box, even as he pushed the lid back with the tips of his thumbs.

The first thing he saw was the platinum Rolex his father had worn the last ten years of his life. It had been a Christmas present from Matt, Mark, and their mom, and the back was engraved, *To Dad, with love.* When the medics had lifted Old Man Murphy's bloated corpse from the floor where Matt and his mom found him, they'd asked if one of them wanted to get the watch… just in case. Obviously it was valuable, and some of the people who stripped the bodies at the morgue could be less than honorable at times. Matt's mom only cried harder, which left him with the duty of removing the watch from his dead father's wrist. And every single day since, he'd cursed his dad for not listening to the doctors when they'd told him he was on his way to a heart attack.

Just beside the watch was a small black velvety box Matt hadn't touched in almost six months—since the day he'd bought the rings inside it, actually. He'd intended on proposing to Brandon that day, but something came up, something he couldn't remember now. Matt did remember the fight they'd had in the days after, because it had been one of the biggest knock-down, drag-outs they'd ever had. Brandon said some pretty cruel shit, things Matt wanted to believe Brandon didn't mean. And Matt had spat back some equally nasty words in return. That had to have been the moment their relationship fell apart, and that was the moment the rings went into the keepsake box and were never taken out again.

Yeah, Matt should've seen that breakup coming....

He reached inside the box, pushed aside the velvet case and his father's watch, and beneath everything was a five-by-seven snapshot of him and Luke—a senior picture of them both in their caps and gowns, rolled diplomas in hand, eager smiles on their faces. They looked so happy, and as far as Matt could remember, they were. Life had yet to break their spirits. Love had yet to break their hearts.

They'd been friends for three years at that point. Luke was new to the school, an import from someplace like California, where the sun always shined and everyone lived on the beach—just like in the movies. Luke had a funny way of saying things, and people didn't warm up to him at first. Not that he wasn't gorgeous enough to fit in with the popular kids; he was just too shy and didn't really try to fit in at all. Like he was too good for the cliques or something, at least the rumors going around the school made it sound as such. Since Matt owned the title of most popular and most loved by... well, everyone, he took Luke under his wing. It just so happened that Luke ended up being the one to teach Matt there was a hell of a lot more to life than being the kid everyone adored, and Matt loved him for it.

Matt always loved him.

He set the box down on the bed but kept the picture in his hands. Luke's golden-blond wisps of hair peeked out from beneath a maroon cap. The maroon-and-white tassel hung down the side of his sun-kissed face, hitting the hard line of his square jaw. Dimples hugged the corners of his lips, and his blue eyes glistened with the truest happiness Matt had ever seen.

"Sunshine," as the cheerleaders called him, contrasted with Matt's not-so-tanned skin, his chin-length caramel hair, and his hazel eyes. Even their personalities contrasted. Matt was the outgoing, goofy flirt, the athlete, and the guy who would cheer for anyone. Luke liked to hide in the shadows and watch the people go by. Sometimes, he even daydreamed, and Matt assumed he was dreaming of being back home, in the salty ocean air and the sunshine and warmth of California as opposed to the gray, smoggy atmosphere of a decaying city like Memphis.

Opposites truly attracted in their case.

Matt traced the impression of Luke's kissable lips with the tip of his thumb, then over one of Luke's dimples. The romantic in him wanted nothing more than to put his clothes back on, turn around, and run back home so he could have his happily ever after with the man he knew deep down in his heart he was meant to be with. The logical side of him knew that would be a dire mistake. Somehow, he knew going back to Memphis would turn a friendship he treasured into a decision he would regret for the rest of his life.

That settled it once and for all. Any desire he'd had to run back home was quickly put to rest, as quickly as he hid the photo away in its safe, special place. He closed the box as a sentiment to the finality of his decision, stood from the bed, and tucked it away in the bottom of his bag where it belonged.

He left out a change of clothes—a pair of boxer briefs, socks, and a T-shirt in one pile, a folded pair of jeans set to the side. Shower tonight, then he'd slip into bed, and tomorrow when he woke up, he could grab his jeans and boots, leather jacket and duffel bag, then hit the road for New Hampshire. He could begin this new chapter of his life.

CHAPTER FIVE

SOMETHING STARTLING woke Matt in the early-morning hours, before the sunlight had a chance to creep in through the edges of the curtains. He bolted straight up in the bed—heart pounding, chest heaving. He felt like he'd been freefalling to his death, but instead of smacking the hard, rough surface of asphalt, he awoke on the billowing cloud of a sagging motel mattress. Yet he still had to pat down his body just to be sure he'd survived the fall.

The details of the dream were scattered in blurry black-and-white images, but he knew he'd seen Brandon and Luke, and he knew neither one of them had appeared to be too happy with him. Matt couldn't remember if it was the look in their eyes or the distance he felt. He only knew the dream left him with an empty, uneasy, and somewhat sorrowful feeling. Made perfect sense in the grand scheme of things. Hell, right now, he assumed no one but his brother, Mark, was happy with him, not even his damn dog.

He rolled off the mattress, stretched his arms and back, then ran his hand down his sweat-dampened sternum. That shower he'd had last night before climbing into bed seemed pretty damn pointless now, but he didn't have time to waste with another one. Mark expected him to be in Portsmouth by a certain time of evening, and if Matt didn't make it, his overly protective big brother would surely send out the search dogs.

As Matt slipped into his jeans, he heard his stomach begin growling, and only then did he remember he hadn't stopped to eat in those ten long hours on the road the day before. Maybe his knotted nerves kept him from noticing his empty gut earlier. Hell, maybe his rumbling stomach was what spooked him out of his dreams this morning. Not that any of that mattered. The pain wouldn't go away until he consumed… something. He had to check out anyway, and most roadside dives had crappy continental breakfast for free in their lobbies. Maybe he could score a bagel or donut or something, maybe a cup of coffee before hitting the road again.

He gave the room one last check as he grabbed his bag from the dresser. Nothing had been left out or left behind. He had his keys, his phone, and his wallet. The wooden box with all his keepsakes was nestled in the bottom of his bag, along with the clothes he'd had on last night. Everything was in its place and ready to go, and for some stupid reason, he didn't want to leave—not to head north, anyway.

Shutting the door behind him, Matt put his game face on and mentally prepared himself for another twelve hours on the road. He mentally prepared himself for the month or two he would be away from everything and everyone he'd ever known and loved—his mom, his pup, his best friend, his home, and his life. It really wasn't too late to turn back. He could call Mark and tell him he changed his mind, that he didn't need time away, that his head was perfectly clear. It would be a lie, but at least he wouldn't have to miss everyone and everything important to him.

This back and forth shit is getting real old, guy.

Yeah. It was.

"Hi, honey," the woman behind the counter called from across the room the moment he stepped through the door. "Ya sure do look a helluva lot better than ya did last night. Take it ya slept well."

"As good as I could," Matt admitted.

"Yeah. This place ain't the Ritz Carlton, but it sure beats drivin' that bike of yours in the rain."

"That it does." Matt laid the key down on the counter and slid it her way.

"You leavin' so soon?"

"Yes, ma'am. My big brother is waiting for me up north."

"Family time is good."

She didn't know it, but he wasn't going there to hang out and socialize with his brother. When it came to the boats and the ocean, Mark always was and always would be all business. After all, "His men have families to get home to." They all trusted Mark's knowledge and attention to detail to keep them safe and bring them back to shore once the season ended.

"I'm going to make a cup of coffee and grab a bagel," Matt finally said as he watched the older woman wobble toward the back of the tiny office area.

"Go right ahead, darlin'. Your receipt'll be right here waitin' for ya."

"Thanks."

A few truckers gathered around a television hanging high in a corner, just above a line of fruits and pastries that had already been plundered. From the looks of it, they didn't care much for the fruit, which was fine by Matt. He preferred a ripe banana to a sugar-coated donut anyway. Their stares followed him as he made his way to the coffee machine. They were giving him a *you-ain't-from-'round-here* look. He kept his eyes straight ahead as he grabbed a tiny Styrofoam cup and poured some coffee—light on the sugar, heavy on the cream. Then he swiped a banana and took a seat at the very back of the tiny makeshift café area.

"They give me the same look," a bass voice said from beside him. The sound came from a tall light-skinned black man with broad shoulders and a thick chest. His shirt was stretched so tight Matt could make out two very rounded pecs. The stranger obviously lifted weights regularly.

"I'm not from around here," Matt said quietly.

"Obviously, neither am I, but with that Southern drawl of yours, I could see you easily being mistaken for a Virginian."

"I'm from Tennessee."

"Beautiful state. What part?"

"Memphis."

"Home of the blues," the guy said with an eager lilt. He smiled so wide his perfect white teeth gleamed in the low light of the room.

"Yeah," Matt said with a crooked grin, just before he took a drink of his coffee. The thick, creamy liquid was so hot it scorched the surface of his tongue and he hissed.

"Be careful. Nothing sucks like losing the feeling in your tongue."

"No kidding," Matt said as he stood from his seat. He lost his craving for coffee and really only wanted to get on the road anyway.

"Hey wait," the stranger stood too. He reached in the back pocket of his jeans and pulled out his wallet. He fished out a business card and handed it over to Matt. "Call me sometime… if you're ever around my way."

Matt looked down at the card. Aric Myers. He had a Connecticut address. "New England, huh? Heading that way myself."

"You going to be there for a while?"

"A few months, maybe longer, but I'm heading out to sea with my brother. He has a fishing boat."

"Nice. Well, when you come ashore again… call me. We'll do lunch or something."

"Sure thing."

Matt tucked the card away in his back pocket, gave the guy a nod, then headed out of the breakfast area, tossing his coffee in a trashcan on his way back to the front counter to get his paperwork.

Admittedly, he thought the encounter with Aric was a little odd. Men didn't normally approach him, not like that. He considered himself ambiguous to anyone who didn't know him. He was rugged, a man's man. Like if that whole gaydar thing was actually a real thing, he didn't trigger any alarms or whatever.

"Thanks," Matt muttered as he swiped the receipt for his room from the counter.

The old woman gave him a genuine smile and told him to have a safe trip. He nodded, then made his way back out to the parking lot where his trusty motorcycle waited to carry him away from his old life.

The sky above him looked like a cracked gray pattern of billowing cotton. The sun glowing up from the horizon cast a pink hue in the distance, an ethereal shade of rose that wound through the collection of clouds. Golden light behind the line of trees made the cityscape look pitch-black. Truthfully, the sight of it made Matt crave that ratty, sagging bed he'd slept on last night, but as badly as he wanted to climb back under the covers, he knew he wouldn't be able to sleep.

He sat down on his bike and rocked it between his legs so he could kick up the stand. His Harley roared to life—V-twin engine rumbling beneath his body. He settled his helmet into place, then gripped the handles tight.

His bike jostled and bounced as it rolled over the cracked and broken driveway and up the on-ramp. Within minutes, though, he was back on the highway, heading northeast toward Philadelphia.

CHAPTER SIX

A LITTLE over fourteen hours and a few too many stops later, Matt pulled into the coastal fishing town of Portsmouth, New Hampshire. The air was brisk, but as clean as anything he'd ever smelled, even with the underlying crispness of salty sea. He parked his bike behind the first building at the edge of the docks, inside a garage—exactly where his brother had told him to during the last call they'd made to each other when Matt had stopped right after leaving New York.

He locked the Harley and fastened his helmet to the seat. Once he had his baby all settled, he wandered out of the garage and out to the docks. Matt didn't have a clue what his brother's boat looked like. Hell, he wasn't 100 percent certain he would know his brother if he saw him. The last time they'd had a face-to-face was about a year before their father's heart attack three years ago. They'd gotten into a big-ass fight over Mark's homophobic wife. Words were thrown back and forth, anger firing from all sides.

Since then, Mark had divorced the wife, and she took custody of his two kids, claiming he wasn't around enough, and his family was a bad influence on their "proper upbringing," or some shit like that. Matt never asked for the details, and Mark never talked about what happened, even during their few and far between phone calls.

Everything was okay now. The reason Mark hadn't come home for their father's funeral was because he'd been at sea, and no one had been able to get ahold of him. Matt's mom flew up there to be with him as soon as he got off the boat, but Matt couldn't make it because he'd been in Jackson, Tennessee, repairing storm damage. They talked about hooking up over the years, but they just couldn't seem to make it happen. One thing or another always seemed to come up.

"Matty!" an old familiar voice with a drawl similar to Matt's called out from the distance. He knew it was Mark, but the setting sun kept him from being able to see his brother's face. The darkened figure waved him over, and Matt started down the pier toward it.

"Mark?"

"Jeez, has it been that long?" His brother met him halfway, arms out for a hug. "You don't recognize me anymore?"

Mark still had the rigid Murphy jawline and their father's eyes—hazel, but more green than brown, sprinkled with a hell of a lot of compassion, because that's how the Murphy men were. Sometimes even caring to a fault. Mark was still as broad in the chest as he'd always been, but now his biceps were so big they looked like they might rip out of his shirt. The sun had bleached his hair so much it had turned a pale, almost dirty-blond color, opposed to the light auburn brown he'd had growing up. Unlike Matt, Mark had cut his hair short, very short.

When they broke away from the reunion hug, Matt reached up and scrubbed his hand over Mark's stubbly scalp. "Shavin' it pretty short these days, aren't you?"

"You will too. It's easier to take care of when you're out on a boat."

"I don't think so, bro. I kinda like my Sampson locks." Matt laughed.

"You'll see."

"Sure. Uh-huh."

They both laughed again, and Mark wrapped his arm over Matt's shoulder and pulled him tight against his side—Mark, the protective big brother. Mark had close to ten years on Matt, and despite those years, they'd always been close. It had a lot more to do with their dad not being around much when they were young than anything else. Just like Matt and Mark, Daddy Murphy's career had kept him away from home most of their lives, but it also afforded them a hell of a lot more luxuries than most kids. And what Matt had lacked in fatherly attention, Mark did his best to make up for.

"You're getting pretty big there, bro," Matt said. "You've about outgrown your clothes."

"Yeah. Yeah. Shrimp." Mark shot him a dimpled grin. "You'll bulk up too. Watch. The first month, everything will ache, and you'll wish you never signed up for this gig. Then when your muscles start to develop, it'll be a breeze."

"You know I'm not a stranger to manual labor, right? You *do* know that I am in construction?"

"Yeah, but construction is nothing compared to the hell of the sea. Just wait. You'll see."

"So when are we heading out?"

"In the next few days. Maybe a week. Depends on the weather. A new storm system formed overnight. Could be bad news for us if we're not careful."

"And you couldn't tell me this when I called from New York? I could've hung around and checked out the sights. I've never been to New York."

"Then you wouldn't have gotten to see me before the work started." Mark squeezed him tighter.

"True."

The ocean clapped against the wooden edges of the pier as they walked farther away from where Matt had parked his bike. The world was loud there—not big city *loud* with the roar of engines and the honking of horns or the sound of machinery grinding away at an empire—but a peaceful sort of loud, the kind that came with crashing ocean waves and seagulls squawking over their heads. The few human voices were almost completely drowned out by nature.

"Hey, Greenhorn, you gonna stand there and daydream, or do you wanna see the boat?"

Matt blinked a few times. He hadn't even realized his brother was no longer beside him. Now Mark stood aboard this huge white-and-green boat with all these metal arms or… something shooting out from the top of it in a Y formation.

"*Murphy's Law?*" Matt asked. "You named your boat *Murphy's Law?*"

"Yeah." Mark shrugged. "What of it?"

"You're a big-ass cornball."

"Yeah. All right. Shut up and climb aboard, Greenhorn."

Matt joined his brother on the boat's deck. He took a look around at all the equipment, and his head started to spin. No way in hell would he ever get the hang of all this. This little life-altering adventure would turn out to be a disaster—he just knew it.

"Dude, what is all that crap?"

"Lobster pots," Mark said, pointing to the wire-cage-looking things. "Live tank," he said, indicating something that looked like a small yet very deep swimming pool. "Sorting table. Over there"—he indicated another set of tubs—"we throw the soft-shell crab over there. They don't make as much as lobster, but they add up pretty fast."

Matt gave him a dumbfounded look.

"Don't worry, little bro. The crew'll help ya get a hang of things. Come on up to the wheelhouse," Mark said, waving Matt up a short flight of steps.

Inside, Matt found even more equipment he couldn't put a name to. He recognized the captain's chair and the steering wheel, a radio and something that looked a lot like a compass, but that was the extent of it. There were gauges and knobs and switches everywhere, a few monitors and windows that looked out over the rest of the boat.

"You know how to use all this crap?" Matt asked.

"Sure do."

He suddenly found a whole new respect for his brother's brand of genius.

"Come on, I'll show you the galley and the cabin," Mark said.

"The galley and the cabin?"

"Where we eat and where we hang out when we aren't working."

"And where do we sleep?"

"Bunks."

"Sounds like summer camp."

Mark chuckled loudly as he led Matt deep into the bowels of the boat. The whole thing reeked of ocean and men who desperately needed to shower. The area was cramped and not the cleanest thing Matt had ever seen. The sight of it made him truly appreciate how much Brandon did at home to keep their place tidy. Matt had gotten very used to that level of cleanliness, and he predicted living in squalor like this boat might eventually get under his skin.

There was a TV hanging on the wall, with a video game console attached to it. It faced away from the bunks toward the bench seat attached to the wall. No more than four feet of space separated the two sides, and Matt assumed sleeping probably didn't happen much when they all got out to sea.

"What's through that door?" Matt asked, pointing to the only other opening in the tiny space.

"Lockers, a shower, and the head. You go through there to get to the engine room. We try to keep the engine room as clean as we can. Two guys get a cleaning shift every other day until we come back to port. It helps keep everything running smoothly."

"Makes sense."

"When the guys get here, they'll show you the ropes, so don't worry, little brother." Mark clapped his hand over Matt's shoulder. "You'll get the hang of it, okay?"

"I'm not looking to make a career out of this, Mark. I just needed a break from life for a little while."

"You plan on telling me what happened?"

Truthfully, no he didn't. He didn't think Mark wanted to hear about the heartbreak of a gay man after his lover ditched him. Not that Mark was judgmental or homophobic, but Mark was also very, very straight. Most straight men didn't want to hear about *anyone's* relationship drama, let alone the drama of a same-sex relationship—at least that's what Matt assumed.

Sighing, he ass-planted on the hunter-green vinyl bench and clamped his hands together between his thighs as he silently put the bits and pieces of the last five years into some sort of coherent order.

"He got sick of my shit," Matt finally said, as if the whole damn situation could be summed up so easily.

"They all get sick of our shit eventually," Mark said, taking the seat beside him. "At least you didn't have too much invested with this guy, right?"

"A house. A pet. A car. I bought him a wedding ring."

"Shit, man. You were going to marry him?"

"Yeah. Bought the ring six months ago."

"So what happened?"

"He got sick of me being gone. Said he wanted a relationship with someone who was around. I told him I couldn't make the money I needed to unless I traveled. So the last time I came back in town, after being gone for three weeks, I came home to an empty house, Zeus in the backyard, and a *Dear John* letter on the dresser."

"Damn, bro, I'm sorry. I don't know what to say."

Matt shrugged. "There really isn't anything to say. He left. It's over."

"Sure is. Time to move on. Seize the day and shit."

"Right."

"C'mon." Mark patted Matt's thigh. "Let's get back on land, get some dinner, and find out what the hell the weather's gonna do."

CHAPTER SEVEN

"SKIPPER!" A high-pitched squeal came from across the bar the moment Matt and Mark darkened the door. Every head in the room turned their way. A tall, thin blonde ran through the center of the room so fast she left a trail of hard wind behind her, hard enough it blew napkins off the tables. She threw her arms around Mark's neck, leapt from her feet, and wrapped her legs around his waist.

"Hey, Emma," he said as he kissed her cheek. Mark held on to her and walked across the room with her attached to his torso. Matt quietly followed them, hoping his brother hadn't forgotten he was back there.

"Oh my God, where have you been?" the Emma person latched on to his brother asked.

Mark carefully pried her off his chest and set her down on a barstool, but he stayed between her legs. He moved in closer, and her denim skirt pushed so far up her thighs Matt could see the red of panties hugging the bottom of her ass cheeks. She leaned in enough he swore her cleavage would flop out of her low-cut shirt.

"I've been dealing with life, babe."

"I hear ya," she said. Then she glanced over Mark's shoulder and spotted Matt. "Who's the cutie ya got with ya, Skipper?"

"That's my baby brother," Mark said, moving over enough to introduce the two of them.

"He don't look like a baby to me."

"I'm not a baby," Matt said flatly.

"Emma. Matt. Matt. Emma." Mark bobbed his head back and forth between them as he said their names. "Emma's my best girl. She takes care of me when I come to Portsmouth."

"And it's my pleasure to do so, darlin'."

"Glad someone is taking care of him," Matt teased. "The guy was always a little overly dependent."

Mark playfully socked Matt in the arm while the blonde practically wrapped around him giggled. She kept her hold on Mark tight, tighter than a normal friend would. She was either vying for his love or trying to make it clear one of them was taken.

Was Mark taken? Again?

Matt gave his brother an arched-brow look of curiosity, one of those *we need to talk* looks. Last thing he'd heard, his brother wasn't in a hurry to get involved with anyone, not after his high-society ex, Constance, ripped out his heart and ran away with the only thing that seemed to make Mark happy. He said he was done with women. They were a pain in the ass.

"Look, honey," Mark said as he eased out of Emma's hold. "My little brother's been on the road for a long time, and he needs to get some food in that belly of his. We're gonna have a seat over by the TV and watch the weather. Can you bring him a big juicy burger or something?"

"No beef," Matt interrupted. "I don't eat red meat."

Mark frowned. "Since when?"

"Since Brandon told me how bad it was for me."

"Brandon. Schmandon. Bring this kid a slab of cow."

"No. Seriously. It'll tear up my stomach. What about grilled fish? I can get that here, right?"

"You don't want fish, bro. You'll be eating more than you can stand while we're on the boat. Bring some steamed veggies and a grilled chicken breast. Sound good."

"Perfect."

The blonde popped up from the barstool and skipped back toward what Matt assumed was the kitchen. Her long curly golden ponytail bounced against her back and trickled down to her waist. Mark watched every single step she took until she disappeared behind the door, and when he turned around and looked at Matt, Matt nearly fell into hysterics.

"Not a word," Mark warned as he started toward the TV.

"Is she special?" Matt asked rather loudly, following his older brother.

Mark took a seat at a corner table, and Matt sat down beside him. He leaned in close and said, "She's trying to be, and she might be getting there. She's the daughter of a lobsterman, so she understands that a guy might have to be out on the water a lot. I get that same reaction every time I see her."

"How long have you guys been dating?"

"I don't know that I would really call it dating, but we've been seeing each other for about a year. She says she can help me get my kids back. She wants to hire a lawyer for me."

"And what's the hold up?"

Mark held up his hand, rubbing the tips of his thumb and forefinger together. He glanced over his shoulder before looking back at Matt and saying, "Money. Last season was bad, bro. I'm still in the red from it. She wants to pay, but—"

"How can a waitress afford to pay for a lawyer powerful enough to get your kids from the claws of the devil herself?"

"She's no waitress."

"Looks like one to me."

"She owns this place."

Matt's mouth formed an O shape. That little revelation came as a shock. Admittedly, he'd judged the book by her cover, and that bouncing blonde came off as nothing more than a cheap romance novel.

"I'd let her pay if she's willing," Matt said. "I mean, dude, it's your kids."

"Yeah, I just don't want her to think I'm using her."

The sound of chairs scooting across the floor made Matt turn around to see what was going on. The weather report had started, and every eye in the joint was trained on the TV. The woman on the screen glided her hand all Vanna White like across the map of New England. Swirling cloud patterns followed behind. Every soul in the joint sat on the edge of their seats, even Mark.

Matt whispered, "What's going on?"

"Looks like the storm might delay us a few more days. Maybe even a week." Mark popped his fist against the table. "Dammit. I really needed that money too."

"So, what are we going to do, then?"

"We could stay here at Emma's place or go to my house in Connecticut. Your choice."

Connecticut, huh?

Matt remembered the card in his back pocket and the handsome man who'd given it to him. No, he wasn't looking for romance, or even a quick lay, not after all the shit he'd been through in the last two weeks. But someone to take his mind off everything, that he could deal with, especially if he was about to have to spend significant time with his brother and who knew how many of his sibling's disgusting friends.

"I'd like to see your place. Mom says it's nice."

"Yeah, and she hasn't seen it since I remodeled."

"Well, sounds like we need to take a little trip."

"Sure do. Connecticut it is, then."

CHAPTER EIGHT

RELUCTANTLY, MATT left his Harley in the garage, which he later found out belonged to Emma as well. Her house spanned the second floor above the bar and carport, and the place was huge, decked out to the nines in nice furniture and all kinds of crazy gadgets Matt couldn't make heads or tails of. Apparently the girl had brains, lots of brains. She did some computer science crap Matt didn't understand and worked in Silicon Valley for a while before her dad passed away and she inherited the family business. The bubbly routine was for the customers... and overdone for Mark.

The black Denali his brother had rode like a Cadillac, even with Mark doing over eighty on the interstate. He talked the entire way, and Matt quietly listened. His brother went on about his misadventures on the high sea, about how the guys were a riot and how Matt would get along well with them. Of course Matt would. He got along with everyone, being Mr. Personality and all. People loved him. He had charisma... or something.

That's what Luke always said, anyway. According to him, Matt should've gone into politics. He could've become president. Matt wasn't an ass-kisser and damn sure wasn't the kind of guy who could sit around in a business suit all day. He enjoyed manual labor, liked to get down and dirty, liked working with his hands. Repairing storm damage made him feel good about himself. While all the other construction workers set out to screw over the victims, Matt would fix them up at about half the cost. He usually went in and did whole neighborhoods, and that's how he made his money. But all that got put on the backburner for a chance to escape everything that reminded him of the man he loved.

"You alive in there?" his brother asked.

Matt had to shake his head just to clear his mind. "Yeah, I'm here."

"Thought you dozed off on me."

"As much as you talk, could've been easy to do."

"We're almost there. Stop your whining."

Matt watched the clear blue Connecticut sky and the lush green wall of trees roll by from the passenger window. For some crazy reason, Luke stayed on his mind. His memory went right back to the moment before the kiss in the kitchen, right before he was going to leave Memphis and Brandon and Luke behind so he could get his head on straight. Matt brushed the tips of his middle and forefinger over his lips. He could almost feel Luke's mouth on his still, could almost feel the explosive warmth all over again.

Luke had asked him if he would've come back home, if the kiss was enough to make him want to stay. If he were completely honest with himself, he would admit to wanting something more than friendship with Luke, but did he want it enough to risk losing Luke if things didn't work out? Almost. The selfish part of him would've given in to the desire and the feelings he'd always had for Luke. But the genuine friend in him, the real man, didn't want to ever lose what he had with Luke, even if it meant they could both finally have the happy ending they deserved.

The problem with Luke was the fact he'd never owned up to any sort of sexuality—straight or bisexual or gay. The kiss threw Matt for a surprise, even though he'd never seen Luke with a girlfriend, or a boyfriend for that matter. Matt always assumed that dating just wasn't important to him, that he had other priorities, and he never bothered to ask his best friend about his sexual orientation. That was a problem because Matt didn't want to get involved—on any level of intimacy—with someone who didn't know what they wanted.

Did Luke know what he wanted? Did Luke swing both ways, or was Matt just a test?

"We're here," Mark said as he swung his Denali into a long gravel driveway.

Matt sat up in the seat, watching as the drive dipped down into a sea of trees. Mark's house hid far from the narrow country road he lived on, and it wasn't until they cleared the seemingly endless rows of trees that Matt finally saw where his brother lived.

The house surprised the hell out of Matt, not that he expected his brother to live in a rat trap, but he damn sure didn't expect a white minimansion and manicured gardens. It was a split-level with a garage at the side closest to the street. The side facing the woods had tall windows that spanned both floors. A deck wrapped around to the side of the house where the door was, and even the door had windows.

"Damn, bro," Matt said. "Didn't expect a place like this. How'd ya score these digs? Thought the ex took you for everything you had."

"She pretty much did. Got to keep my ride. The house, I got it for a steal, but it was falling apart. Took a hell of a lot of work to make her look this good. She's right at thirty-five hundred square feet. Five bedrooms. Three bathrooms. Nice kitchen and a sunroom looking out into the forest. There's even a tiny lake around back. It's nice here. Quiet."

"I can tell."

"I still have some work to do. I haven't even started on the upstairs, but she's livable."

"Well, if you want to get a little work done while we're here, construction is my specialty."

"Might have to take you up on that, man."

Mark parked the Denali in front of the garage. He didn't bother lifting the door to pull inside, and with a ride like that, Matt wondered why he wouldn't want to keep it safe, especially with a storm coming. He didn't ask why his brother chose to leave it out in the elements. Mark probably had a few project cars in the garage anyway. He had a thing for fixer-uppers—houses, cars… women.

They both hopped out of the truck. Matt reached in the back to grab his bag, and then he followed his brother to the door. The inside of the house was just as amazing as the outside. They entered a foyer first—a narrow hallway lined with russet-colored tiles and crème-colored walls, complete with a stark white chair rail and elaborate crown-molding. A sepia print of him and Matt as children hung on the wall. Matt remembered that picture, and seeing it enlarged and professionally framed gave him a warm and fuzzy feeling. It was good to know that despite the differences they'd had in the past, Mark still wanted their best picture put on display so proudly.

The foyer spilled into a kitchen with the same tiles and walls. The cabinets were a mahogany color and the countertops were the same shade of brown as the floors. The appliances were all stainless steel, and not cheap shit, just like the overhead lighting. Matt was more than familiar with the style. He'd used it in a few higher-end homes.

"You chose a great palette," Matt said.

"Emma helped."

"That's cool."

"Yeah, she has great taste," Mark said as he opened the refrigerator door. He reached inside and grabbed a beer, handed one to Matt, then got one for himself. "I have some frozen dinners in here if you're hungry or whatever."

"Still can't cook for shit, huh?" Matt laughed.

"Nope."

"Neither can I. Brandon did all of our cooking."

"Constance did ours. So, dinner?"

"Nah, I think I'll pass. I'm still stuffed from the food Emma fed me." Matt settled against the kitchen counter, arms crossed over his chest. He watched his brother down half the beer in his hand. "I think I might try to have plans tomorrow. Is that cool with you?"

"Plans? Who do you know in Connecticut?"

A crooked smile lifted one corner of Matt's lips. He took a long swig of his beer before he dared to answer his brother. He didn't want to hear any lectures about running off in the night with some random stranger. He'd gotten that lecture more than once back when they all lived back at home as one big, happy family.

"Someone I met in Virginia," he finally said. "Might meet him somewhere tomorrow, just to get away for a bit. Could I borrow your truck if I can meet up with him?"

"Sure thing. Just, be careful, okay?"

"Yeah. Yeah. Let me call him and see what's up before I try to make definite plans."

"Okay. Well, how about I show you to your room?"

"Sounds great."

CHAPTER NINE

AT THE end of a long hall was a collection of bedrooms and a bathroom. One room was Mark's, and the other had been designated as a guest bedroom. Matt half expected there to be no furniture. He half expected the room to be in shambles, but what he found surprised him… yet again. His brother seemed to be surprising him a lot.

The walls were pale gray, and the hardwood floors were polished to a high shine. They were light like bamboo and contrasted the mocha-colored furniture nicely. A white down comforter covered the bed. A row of three huge windows faced the front yard and its gorgeous gardens. A black-and-white print of an old ship hung over the chest of drawers.

Matt set his duffel bag on a black chaise lounge sitting catty-corner in front of the windows, and then he looked back at his brother. "This is great, man. I really like it here. I could be comfortable in a place like this."

"You know you don't have to leave once we get back to shore. I mean, I have this entire place to myself, and it's entirely too much space for one man."

"I have a dog back home."

"We can go get him."

"What about Mom?"

"I'm trying to get her to move up here. She's too old to be living alone in Memphis. It's too dangerous for her."

Matt certainly agreed, but why the hell hadn't Mark talked to him about his plans to get their mother up north? It bothered him that he hadn't been let in on the plan by his brother nor his mom. He wouldn't make a stink about it, not right now. There wasn't much sense in getting into an argument with his brother, especially with Matt being stranded there.

"So, um… make yourself at home," Mark said. "I'm going to hit the hay."

"Night, bro."

"Night."

Mark closed the door behind himself, and when the knob jiggled into place, Matt reached for the business card he'd shoved in his pocket back in Virginia. The moment he read Aric's name, he remembered the man's smooth, rich voice and his incredible smile.

So calling Aric could end up being a complete waste of time, not that Matt wanted anything in particular, nothing more than someone to talk to and hang out with, especially if he was going to be stuck in Connecticut for the next week. He knew if he ended up with no one other than Mark to talk to, his mind would wander right back to Brandon's breakup and Luke's kiss. He would probably spend the entire week sulking, maybe even drowning his misery in beer.

He shrugged out of his leather jacket and laid it down next to his duffel bag, then fished his phone out of his pocket. One by one, he entered the numbers on the card, then waited to hear that wonderfully sultry voice of Aric's to answer on the other end.

"Hello?" Aric said.

"Hey, um… this is Matt—the guy you met in Virginia," assuming Aric would remember, that he didn't hand out his card to every stranger he met.

"Matt. Hello." Aric sounded both surprised and happy to hear Matt's voice. "I didn't expect to hear from you again."

"I'm in Connecticut. There was a slight change of plans."

"Slight, huh?"

"Yeah. The storm is keeping us inland for another week. I'm at my brother's house."

"I got back home this morning."

"That's cool."

"Yes, it is, isn't it?"

"Yeah, sure is."

"Did you want something from me?"

"I, um… I didn't want to stay cooped up in the house with my brother all week." Matt sat down on the edge of the bed as he held the phone in one hand and ran the other through his light brown hair. No matter how many times he brushed it back, it still fell down to his chin. "I was thinking about getting out tomorrow, but I don't know my way around and really don't want to go alone."

"Were you looking for a tour guide or someone to join you?"

"Someone to join me, if you'd like to."

"I think we can make that happen."

"We need to go someplace casual. I didn't bring a whole lot of clothes with me, and I'm not sure what Mark has. He's already gone to bed."

"I can do casual. I rather enjoy casual."

"Perfect."

"So," Aric said, "what time would you like to meet tomorrow?"

"I don't know. Early evening maybe?"

"How about five? Does that sound okay to you?"

"Sounds great. That'll give me time to hang out with my brother so it doesn't look like I'm ditching him."

"Perfect. I'm looking forward to it, Memphis."

"Sounds great. See you tomorrow."

As Matt hung up the phone, he silently wondered what the hell he was doing, why he even considering going out to meet a man he didn't know, a man he'd only met yesterday. Had Matt finally lost his mind?

Laughing, he shook his head, pushed up from the bed, and crossed the room to his duffel bag. He dug through the bag for his brush, cologne, deodorant, and a few other toiletries. He planned to take a shower, then hit the hay. Maybe get a good night's rest since he hadn't had a decent night's sleep in far too long. He sure as hell didn't want to climb into a clean bed the way he smelled right now. The hours spent on the road had him smelling vaguely similar to diesel exhaust. That was one of the downfalls of spending so many hours on a highway with a ton of semis and no glass and metal to save him from the fumes, and frankly, the stench was a bit rank.

When Matt stepped into the hallway, he heard clanking and shuffling coming from the direction of the kitchen. He thought his brother had gone to bed, but maybe Mark was a light sleeper just like Matt. He headed down the hall calling his brother's name as he approached.

"Mark? You there?"

"Yeah. I'm in the kitchen."

Matt rounded the corner and found his brother dumping the contents of a Chinese carton onto a plate. It looked like some sort of meat and noodle dish. "Is that stuff safe to eat?"

"I just bought it yesterday." Mark brought the carton to his nose and took a deep whiff. "Yep. Still good."

"That's just great." Matt laughed. "Look, I apparently didn't bring enough clothes with me. I planned on just needing ratty jeans and T-shirts for the boat. I didn't expect to need something decent. You mind if I borrow something to wear for tomorrow?"

"Sure. Help yourself to my closet. Take anything you want."

"Thanks, bro."

Matt turned to leave, but his brother's voice stopped him. "So, you're really going out tomorrow?"

"Yeah, that's the plan. Why?"

"Just be careful, 'kay? You don't know nothin' 'bout this guy. Just… watch your back."

"I plan to," Matt said. He waited for his brother to go into a diatribe about making smart decisions and how people couldn't be trusted, but thankfully, Mark never did. Thankfully. "Thanks again for the clothes."

"No problem."

Matt left his brother in the kitchen, tending to his leftovers and nursing a sweaty bottle of beer. He almost felt bad for running out on the guy, but if he stayed there, staring at the ceiling and letting his mind ramble, Matt knew he would go insane. Tomorrow, he would have to get out of there simply because Matt tended to be restless like that. Even if Mark didn't like him leaving, even if Mark had his reasons for being leery, Matt knew he would need to roam.

Mark never liked to talk about it, but a few years before Matt had been born, their older brother, Jacob, had been violently taken from the world, and the details of their sibling's death remained unclear to this day. And that's why Mark had always been so paranoid and protective of Matt.

Mark was almost eight when it happened. It was two days before Jacob's thirteenth birthday. He wanted to play in the park, and their parents promised to take the boys, but things kept coming up. Their father had to leave town all the time, and it left a lot of responsibility for maintaining the house on their mother. Things happened, and quality time with the boys fell through the cracks more often than not.

Well, one afternoon, Jacob hopped on his bike and headed to the park alone. Mark had been in his bedroom playing with who knew what when Jacob left. Their mother called the boys to the kitchen for lunch, but Jacob never showed.

Jacob's body had been found in the woods just beyond the park nearly three days after the boy had been reported missing. The police never caught the guy who'd strangled the life out of twelve-year-old Jacob Murphy, and he was the brother Matt would never know, the one lingering darkness no one in the family ever really wanted to talk about. Matt hadn't even known about Jacob until he was close to fifteen, and only then because he'd found a picture of Mark and an older boy who looked a hell of a lot like the two of them. Seventeen years had passed since Jacob's death, and still their mother had a hard time broaching the subject. Still, Mark doubted every stranger and protected his brother like Matt was the next prophet or something.

Long story short, everyone was always particularly protective of Matt, even as Matt grew into adulthood, and running out to meet some strange man definitely put his brother on edge.

CHAPTER TEN

THE NEXT day, Matt woke up renewed. The sleep he'd gotten had been a godsend. He felt so good he helped Mark make a few repairs to the house before the time came for him to get cleaned up and head into the city to meet Aric.

With his body clean and smelling like the cologne he'd loved since puberty, back when it became important to smell his best *all* the damn time, Matt headed out of his bedroom and on to the kitchen. He grabbed the keys off the hook and yelled back at Mark, "I'll be back later." Mark grumbled something in return.

Aric had texted him the address of the restaurant, and it took almost an hour to get to that part of town. That neck of the woods was much busier than Mark's little country corner of Connecticut, but nowhere near as bustling as Memphis. Finding the place wasn't a problem. Parking wasn't a problem. Again, a luxury he didn't have back home.

Waiting outside the restaurant, Matt smoothed his hands down the front of the khaki slacks he'd borrowed from his older brother. They were a little too big but didn't look bad on him. Neither did the crimson dress shirt and the brown leather oxfords. He had a feeling Constance had picked those clothes for Mark, because Mark would've never worn anything so conservative, and the idea of that almost made Matt's stomach turn. Or was it the nervousness of meeting up with someone he didn't really know?

A silver BMW M3 with dark tinted windows pulled to a stop in front of him. The headlights blinded him, and he shielded his eyes with the length of his forearm as he turned his head to the side. The lights died, and Aric emerged from the driver's side. He wore a long-sleeved, azure dress shirt and black tie, black slacks, and black shoes. His hair looked a lot shorter than it was when they'd first met, and he didn't have an inch of stubble on his cheeks.

Aric stepped forward with his hand extended and a smile curling his light brown lips. He took Matt's hand and gripped it hard, giving him a firm handshake, as if they were potential partners, meeting to discuss official business and nothing more. And that still didn't answer the question of his sexuality.

"I'm glad you called," Aric said as he released Matt's hand. "I thought I would be spending the evening in front of the TV."

"Yeah, I thought I would be in the middle of the Atlantic Ocean right now."

"You sound disappointed."

"In a way, I am. This little adventure was supposed to get my mind off things, not give me time to do more thinking."

"Shall we fix that with a bit of conversation and a delicious meal?"

"I think that sounds like a great idea."

Aric nodded; then he reached for the brass handle of the restaurant's front door. He held it open and waited for Matt to step inside. The hostess greeted them with a smile, and Matt asked for a table for two. As she made her way to the back of the restaurant, her auburn ponytail bounced against the back of her white dress shirt. Matt was very aware of Aric's closeness, not only from the sweet but manly scent of his cologne, but from the feeling of Aric's brown eyes staring into the back of his neck.

"Is this okay?" the hostess asked, standing next to a rounded booth in the back.

"This will be just fine," Aric said.

Matt sat down first, and Aric joined him, taking the spot directly across from Matt on the same horseshoe-shaped bench. If they decided over the course of their meal to get a little closer, that spot would allow for it without being too obvious. Before they even settled into their seats, a waiter appeared with a basket of bread and a wine list.

"Bring us a bottle of a nice Chianti and two glasses, please?" Aric asked, pressing his palm toward the wine list. The waiter tucked it under his arm and smiled. "I hope you like wine."

"I do. I'm no connoisseur or anything, but I've never had a wine I didn't like."

"This is a very aromatic wine. Rich but great with Italian food."

"I'll just have to trust you." Matt grinned crookedly.

Aric reached up and grabbed the triangle of folded maroon napkin from the center of the appetizer plate, snapped it loose, and laid it across his thighs. Matt couldn't help but watch him. There was an elegance to his movement, a smoothness in everything he did.

The waiter came back with the bottle and two glasses Aric had asked for. He presented the bottle and Aric nodded his approval. The waiter then placed a glass in front of each man. He poured the deep red wine into each glass and asked them if they were ready to order.

"I'll have the veal parmigiana with steamed mushrooms," Aric said.

"I'll just have some um…." Matt glanced over the menu for the first time. The no-beef kick he'd been on didn't work well in this situation. He didn't immediately see anything he could have. "Do you have some sort of shrimp alfredo?"

"We do," the waiter said.

"That's what I'll have."

"Good choice."

The waiter took their menus and promptly disappeared into the shadows of the low-lit restaurant. Matt's gaze followed the kid, just because it seemed a hell of a lot more appropriate than gawking at Aric.

"So tell me," Aric said, and the sound of his voice pulled Matt away from his staring. "What *things* are you trying to get off your mind, if I may ask?"

"I um…." Matt took a breath as he ran his fingers through his hair. "A five-year relationship that ended with a Dear John letter."

"That was kind," Aric said sarcastically. "And why did this person leave you?"

"I'm not at home enough. They said they needed more."

"They did, did *they*?"

"Yeah. We had a life together, a house, and a dog. I bought them a ring and everything."

"And *he* couldn't stand not having you around?"

Matt didn't answer the question. Mostly because the pain of what had happened to him in Memphis was still a bit too raw and just thinking about it tightened his throat.

"Did I overstep my bounds?" Aric asked.

"No." Matt shook his head. "No."

"Is it too soon? Dating, I mean?"

Not really. Okay, maybe a little?

"This is all just really weird to me. I was in a relationship for a really long time and—" Matt frowned. "Well, I also never got asked out on dates."

"Why?"

"Because people don't normally catch on… you know, to me being gay. I mean, I don't fit the stereotypes, I guess."

Aric arched a brow. Jeez, had Matt offended him already?

"That probably sounds bad, but… I don't know. Maybe I should shut up now."

Aric laughed softly. "No. I wasn't certain when I gave you my card. I thought you were handsome, and I hoped we played for the same team. When you took it, I thought *maybe*… but when you called me, my suspicions were confirmed. I must admit, I was excited to hear your voice."

"I'm not looking for anything right now," Matt blurted.

Aric took a sip of his wine, swallowed, then took another. "I didn't assume you were." He set the glass back down and immediately folded his hands in his lap. "I'm not looking for anything either. Well, nothing serious anyway."

The uncomfortable conversation lulled into awkward silence. They both casually drank wine and snacked on bread. If neither one of them was looking for anything, why in the hell did Aric give Matt his card, and why in the hell did Matt call him? Christ, he needed to stop overthinking this. He couldn't help it, though. He hadn't been in the dating game in half a decade and wasn't sure if the rules had changed.

"Hmm… I must've dampened the mood," Aric said.

"No. No, you didn't. I just—" Matt laughed nervously. "—have no clue what I'm doing here. I don't know what I was thinking or what I was looking for."

"Relax, Matt. Just enjoy the company."

"You're right. I'm being ridiculous."

The waiter came back with their food. Matt and Aric were in the middle of laughing over their shared ignorance to the ways of single life and the nonhetero dating scene. Aric confessed he'd just come out of a ten-year relationship himself. His ex-partner had been eighteen years old when they started dating. Aric was seven years his senior. Eventually, their tastes had changed, and they'd grown apart. Aric said he'd sworn off anyone under thirty from that point on. Matt laughed. He was just far enough over the mark that Aric didn't seem to have a problem with his age.

The moment the waiter sat their food down, conversation halted, and both men took to stuffing their faces, albeit Aric did it with much more class than Matt did. Matt acted like he hadn't eaten in ages.

"Hungry?" Aric asked, laughing softly as he wiped the edges of his lips.

Heat rushed Matt's face. "I'm embarrassing myself, aren't I?"

"It's adorable, sweetie."

"Ha!" Matt snorted. He sat down his fork and wiped the creamy sauce from his lips. "Brandon hated my scarfing, said it lacked class."

"Was there anything he actually liked about you?"

"Ya know, I have no clue. The first few years we were together, he never complained about anything. In fact, I think the complaining didn't start until about six months ago, right after I bought the rings."

"Did he know about the rings?"

"I don't think so, not unless he found them. I have this little treasure chest thing I made in my high school shop class. I keep everything sentimental in it. Unless he went searching through the box, he wouldn't have known about them."

"Would he search your private things?"

"I don't know. Maybe?"

"Maybe."

Aric pushed his empty plate across the table, then poured himself another glass of wine. He offered Matt more Chianti, and Matt shook his head as he swallowed down the last of his pasta. "I have to drive back to my brother's house tonight," he said. "It's a pretty far drive."

"You could always sober up at my place. I live a few blocks away."

Oh, but wasn't that a wonderfully stupid idea? Get drunk, then go home with a man he didn't know, a man who admitted his attraction to Matt, who wasn't looking for anything meaningful but would probably take a quick lay in a heartbeat. And the more he sat there staring at Aric's strong jawline and smooth brown lips, the more appealing the idea of going home with him became.

"I shouldn't," Matt finally said.

"I promise I have nothing lascivious in mind."

"But I don't know you."

"We're just two men who had a little too much wine. Two men who wanted to finish our conversation. Two men who were looking for company."

Matt took another long sip of his wine, finishing what was left in the glass. He looked back over at Aric, and in a breathy voice, he said, "Lead the way."

CHAPTER ELEVEN

ARIC'S HOME was quite literally three city blocks away from the restaurant. It wasn't some over-the-top Connecticut mansion, though Matt assumed Aric could probably afford one if he wanted, judging by the car he drove and the AmEx Black card he'd thrown down on their two-hundred-dollar meal. Distantly, Matt wondered how in the hell Aric had ended up in that dive motel back in Virginia and why he hadn't been staying somewhere more high class.

The fall night was biting against Matt's cheeks the moment he climbed out of his brother's Denali. It wasn't the kind of fall they had back in Tennessee but a hell of a lot cooler, windier even.

"Nice place," Matt said as he stared up at the two-story colonial with a zero-lot line. It looked like an older home with modern windows and doors, with uplights that put the house on display in the middle of the night. Beds of evergreens surrounded the full-length porch.

"It belonged to my mother. She loved the place and desperately wanted to keep it in the family. That's the only reason I came back to Connecticut."

"Came back from where?"

"New York," Aric said as he slid his key into the lock and opened the door. He reached in and turned on the lights, then held the door open and waited for Matt.

"What did you do in New York?" Matt asked as he stepped inside.

"Investment banking. Rich people pay me a lot of money to intelligently spend everything they have. I have a great track record for picking investments that pay off."

"My brother could use an investor," Matt muttered. Obviously Aric didn't hear him or didn't pay him any attention.

Aric led them out of the foyer and into a living room, and he made sure to turn on the light just before Matt stumbled down the two short steps and landed on his face. "Thanks," he said as he stepped down.

The room had the same contemporary, minimalist style Matt's former home back in Tennessee had. It was still warm and inviting, but not overcrowded. Aric chose an earthy palette with dark woods and dark leather to decorate his home. The wall hangings were mostly black-and-white prints. And the golden lighting above cast a soft glow on every dark surface.

Seeing it all took him back to the day he and Brandon had decided to work on their home. Matt had handed Brandon the credit card and told him to have fun. Matt didn't have a clue when it came to design, but he knew quality fixtures and good craftsmanship, but making things visually appealing had always been Brandon's job.

"You're quiet," Aric said as he turned away from a bar in the far corner of the room. He'd poured two more glasses of wine while Matt wasn't looking. It was a red, just like they'd had at dinner.

"Had something on my mind," Matt said, taking the glass Aric offered him, though Aric's fingers lingered a little longer than necessary, and Matt didn't immediately pull away.

Matt cleared his throat as he met Aric's intense dark stare. The closeness was just as awkward and uncomfortable as it was exciting. Despite Matt's not looking for any sort of intimacy from anyone, he felt drawn to Aric, drawn to the mystique behind Aric.

"Would it be over the line if I kissed you?" Aric whispered as he reached up with his free hand to touch Matt's cheek.

The warmth of Aric's palm made Matt close his eyes. He licked his dry lips and leaned in a little closer. "Not at all," Matt breathed.

The moment the words cleared his mouth, he felt Aric's lips lightly brush against his. It started out chaste yet sensual, delicate and tender. Without pulling away, Aric set his glass of wine down on the bar, then took Matt's and did the same. His grace was absolutely flawless, something that reminded Matt of being with Brandon. Even Aric's slightly smaller yet muscled frame so close to Matt's broad form reminded him of Brandon.

He felt Aric's tongue swipe over his lips, and Matt opened his mouth a little wider. It was a natural response, as if Matt's body knew what it needed and wanted, despite Matt's mind and heart knowing a very, very different truth. He wasn't ready to move on from Brandon, hence the reason he'd bolted after Luke kissed him.

Even as he silently struggled over timing and the affairs of his heart, he welcomed Aric's affection. Their lips caressed, slowly opening and closing as the kiss deepened. Aric dipped his tongue deep into Matt's mouth, licking the roof and twisting with Matt's. The feel of it made Matt purr, and by the time he'd realized the sound wasn't simply in his head, it was too late to stop it.

Matt pulled back, breaking the seal of their lips. His eyes partially opened, though his stare remained hooded. Aric brushed his thumb over Matt's cheek and smiled. "Why did you stop me so soon?" Aric asked.

"Because this is wrong," Matt said with a certain bit of finality.

"Why is it wrong?" Aric took another step backward, obviously to give Matt space or maybe to give himself the space he needed. Disappointment swept over his face. "We're two grown, single men. There are no strings and no expectations, and that was simply a kiss."

"Because I couldn't stop thinking about Brandon. You're about his size, and you kiss just like him. It um… just put me in a weird place."

"Then why don't we forego the kissing and simply keep each other company? Is that something you can do?"

"I think I can."

"Then have a seat on the couch, and I'll start the fire."

Matt took a spot on one of the matching sofas. The leather creaked as he sat down. He did his best to get comfortable, but it seemed the more he tried, the more uncomfortable he became. Aric was nice and the type of guy Matt would go for in a heartbeat, but he was too much like Brandon, and Matt couldn't see any possible relationship with him lasting too long. He didn't want to get wrapped up in anything like that again. He didn't want to have his heart broken and damn sure wasn't ready to consider falling in love.

And yes, he knew he was overthinking the situation. His mind moved on from first dates and first kisses, straight to fighting for blankets and time in the bathroom, holidays spent with families, and shared bank accounts. The thought made him freak out so bad he began fidgeting with his fingers just so they wouldn't shake.

Aric got the heat going. It wasn't a traditional wood-burning fireplace, but rather gas, and while it took little effort, Matt preferred the smell of pine burning in an open flame. It reminded him of Christmases spent in Tennessee during his childhood, of a time when the family felt whole, despite the death of the firstborn son all those years before Matt's birth.

"Perfect," Aric said as he took a step back from the fireplace. He rubbed his hands together, then spun on his heel and smiled at Matt. "It's cozy."

"Yeah, it is." Matt gave a crooked grin as Aric sat down beside him.

There was enough distance between them that Matt felt like he could relax again. He let out a long, slow breath and dropped his hands to his lap.

"I must admit," Aric said, "you're even more handsome in this light than you were before."

Matt opened his mouth to say something but quickly closed it. Truthfully, Aric was pretty damn gorgeous in that light too. The flames flickering behind him cast an amber glow on his mocha-colored skin. They accentuated the strength and firmness of his jawline and made his kiss-moistened lips glisten. The sight made Matt want to kiss Aric again, even though his brain screamed about the whole situation being a horrible mistake.

"What's on your mind?" Aric asked in a quiet, sincere voice.

"My mind is all over the place right now," Matt said. "Honestly, it's at war with itself."

"And what is this war about?"

"Kissing you. Not kissing you."

Aric frowned. "Are you trying to convince yourself you don't want to?"

"Sort of. I know what kissing leads to. I know it's wrong for me to think about someone else while your lips are on mine. I know if it went any further, I would be thinking about Brandon, and that's not fair to you."

"What do *you* want?" Aric asked as he reached for Matt's hand.

Their fingers locked, and Aric didn't push any further than holding hands. He obviously wouldn't push for anything more than Matt was willing to give, and didn't that earn him something, even if that something was a small, intimate gesture like a kiss?

For once, Matt planned to ignore his heart and listen to his body's needs.

Turning on the couch, he still held Aric's hand and lifted up to his knees. He leaned forward, pressing his body against Aric's, and they met in another kiss. Only this time, the kiss was immediate and more heated than the first one. His tongue dove deep into Aric's mouth, and his body blanketed Aric's muscled form. He felt Aric's arms wrap around his waist and two strong hands dip down into the back of his khaki slacks. Those thick fingers gripped at Matt's ass, fingertips biting into muscle. The feel of it made Matt moan into Aric's mouth.

Matt pushed his hips between Aric's thighs, grinding against them as their lips caressed and their tongues made love to each other's mouths. The idea of being with someone this way excited him. He hadn't touched any other man but Brandon in five years, and Matt found himself craving the newness of the experience, despite his urgent need not to get involved with another person the way he had been with Brandon.

Matt simply stopped fighting and let his body take control.

CHAPTER TWELVE

"CONDOM?" MATT rasped as they stumbled away from the couch and closer to the fire. Aric's lips hadn't left Matt's throat. He kissed his skin raw, teasing and toying and nipping at the delicate flesh of Matt's neck. Aric had one hand locked over Matt's groin, fingers waving and massaging, rousing him to the hardest Matt had been in a very long time.

"Get undressed," Aric breathed against Matt's ear. "I'll be right back."

With trembling fingers on his belt buckle, Matt watched as Aric raced from the living room. He let his head roll back, eyes trained on the flat matte ceiling as he slowed his breathing and licked his parched lips. He silently encouraged himself, chanting over and over again that everything would be okay and he needed to do this. He needed to let go and give in to the desires of the flesh, let the feel of another man's body against his make him forget everything he'd been running away from. Matt wasn't the kind of guy who got into casual sex, but this time, he thought he could be.

He unbuckled his belt as he kicked away his shoes, unzipped his pants and shimmied until the fabric pooled at his ankles. His rock-hard erection sprang free, standing at full salute and eager as hell to feel Aric's warm ass surrounding it. He gripped his cock and balls, massaging roughly as he took to the buttons of his dress shirt with his free hand. He fumbled the first one loose, then another and another, but it wasn't going fast enough. If he wanted to be completely naked by the time Aric came back, he would have to use both hands, yet he didn't want to let go of his erection. The pressure felt good. Too good.

Aric reappeared in all his naked glory—fully aroused, with a bottle of lube in one hand and a condom in the other. The fire cast a golden sheen over the mounds of muscle rippling down the length of his body. A trail of pitch-black curls shadowed the crease above his navel, then dipped down, forming an arrow-like shape that directed Matt's stare to a long, thick—and completely erect—cock.

"Need some help?" Aric teased.

Matt bit down hard on his bottom lip as Aric slowly approached him.

In passing, Aric set the lube and condom on the end table, then continued toward Matt. He stood close enough their erections pressed together, and Matt immediately removed his hand from his own crotch and turned the attention to Aric's.

Aric moaned as Matt began to slowly stroke him. His hands shook as he fought to unbutton Matt's shirt. "Christ, you're huge," Matt whispered. Aric gave him a wicked grin and lowered his head to the curve of Matt's neck. He felt Aric's full lips lock over his collarbone—teeth fondling the firm ridge, tongue licking across his moist skin.

The soft fabric of Matt's shirt caused a chill to ripple down his body as it slid over his arms. He let the shirt drop to the floor, landing wherever the hell it wanted.

"Are you down for a little oral?" Aric asked as he lowered himself to the floor.

He knelt in front of Matt, kissing playful circles over Matt's chest, running his hands over Matt's thighs. The best Matt could manage was a moan, a sound that meant Aric could have his cock in any way he wanted as long as it led to relieving some of the pressure in Matt's balls.

The moment the moist heat of Aric's mouth sheathed his shaft, Matt's eyes closed, and his head rolled back. His legs started to quiver, and his chest heaved with every labored breath he took. There was something enchanting and mind-numbing about the way Aric traced the length of his erection with the firm tip of his tongue. The way he took Matt to the hilt without even choking was something Matt hadn't experienced before and didn't put much stock in until he felt the waving muscles of Aric's throat as he swallowed him down.

"Holy shit," Matt gasped as he reached down and palmed the back of Aric's head. Aric's moans vibrated the sensitive skin of his cock and tickled those already alert nerves. Aric pulled back, ran his tongue around and around the head of Matt's cock, around and around before swallowing him whole again. The sensations were only intensified by the feel of Aric's strong fingers massaging his sac.

"Don't stop. God, don't stop," Matt moaned.

Suddenly he felt another hand cradling his ass. One finger stroked up and down the valley between his cheeks. Aric teased him, circling that one finger around his puckered opening, applying enough pressure to draw Matt's sac tighter against his body. "I'm about to come," he said. "I swear to God, I'm about to—"

Aric didn't stop. His head bobbed faster, fingers gripping Matt's sac tighter. Matt rolled his hips, pulling back and pushing his cock deep into Aric's mouth again. Then Aric began to ease his thick finger into Matt's ass.

Every muscle in Matt's body tensed. He let out a growl that rumbled up his chest and vibrated his throat. Aric took it slow, stroking in and out at half the pace of his bobbing head. The combined feel of it all—the way Aric's tongue encircled his shaft, the way his fingertip brushed the right spot, the way his hand felt on Matt's sac—almost did Matt in. But right before that glorious moment, before the orgasm and an early end to the night, Aric pulled back. Cool air gusted over Matt's cock. He rolled open his eyes and found his new friend licking his glistening bottom lip.

"You taste as good as you smell." Aric reached down and gripped himself, hungrily gazing up. "See how hard I am for you?"

"Lie down," Matt said hoarsely, pointing at the floor close to the fire. Aric gave him a wicked grin and immediately settled onto his stomach, glorious ass poking up from the floor.

Matt kept his eyes on the fire glistening in the layer of sweat coating Aric' muscles. He kept one hand on his cock, slowly stroking as he eyed Aric's backside.

"Roll over," he said. "I want to see your face when I make you come."

Aric did as Matt commanded. He rolled over—one leg bent, foot pressed against the floor, showing off his exquisite endowment. Matt grabbed the little foil square from the end table, put one corner between his teeth, and tore the package open like a rabid animal ready to devour the first meal it'd had in weeks. He rolled the rubber down his shaft, then grabbed the bottle of lube and carried it over to where Aric lay.

Kneeling down, Matt positioned himself between Aric's muscled thighs. He squeezed the lube onto his palm and wrapped his hand around his cock and began to stroke as he bowed down to press kisses on Aric's chest. Aric's skin tasted like honey, like a sweet and salty, sultry mix of whatever lotion he used and the sweat clinging to his flesh.

He pressed the head of his cock to Aric's opening, gentle pressure at first because Aric was new to him, and he didn't know how often Aric played bottom to a top like Matt. He didn't know if Aric could handle his girth or if this would be one of those "take it easy" type of situations. But the moment the head of Matt's cock met the ring of muscle buried in Aric's gloriously rounded ass, Aric lifted his body to angle himself for penetration.

"Give it to me, Matt," Aric said, eyes fluttering. He licked his lips and rolled his head, arched his back and spread his thighs wider. "I can handle it, baby. Just stop teasing."

"Oh, but teasing is half the fun," Matt said as he pushed the first few inches into Aric's body.

Slow, easy movement, he let Aric marinate in the feel of those few short strokes, and he listened as Aric whimpered and panted. Matt's arms tensed as he pressed his palms to the floor at either side of Aric's face. He held himself inches from Aric's lips, breathing deep enough for Aric to feel each soft gust of wind as Matt exhaled.

"You're going to drive me insane," Aric said, lifting his lower body and forcing more of Matt's cock inside him. The feel of it was almost enough to make Matt give in.

"Easy," Matt said, pulling back again.

"No. Not easy. Jesus Christ, Matt, fuck me. Please. Fuck. Me."

"I like the way you beg for it. I like the way you want it so badly."

"You cruel, cruel tease."

"Yes, but you're enjoying it, aren't you."

"God help me, yes. Yes, I am."

With that last winded phrase, Matt pulled out and lifted himself up until he was kneeling again. He gripped Aric's calves and pushed Aric's legs into the air, rolling him back, exposing that tight warm opening until Matt had clear aim to slide right in. He knew Aric's body could handle his girth, had felt it when Aric so easily forced him deeper. Matt kissed the side of Aric's leg and slowly pushed every inch of his cock into Aric's body.

As he pulled back slowly, Aric's winded pleas filled the air and made a new wave of excitement trickle through Matt. It was the first time he'd been with someone so vocal, and the more Aric praised his prowess, the more Matt wanted to make him enjoy it. He liked those airy moans and ragged words, loved the way Aric prayed to God for more.

He pumped against Aric's body, pulling back slowly, then thrusting his many thick inches deep inside again. Every pass made Aric writhe beneath him, made him clench his jaw tighter. And every time Matt pulled out, Aric opened his eyes and silently begged for more.

The last sudden thrust made Aric cry out Matt's name. A heated burst of pearly streams erupted from the head of Aric's cock and coated Matt's stomach. Matt had hit the right spot, had stroked the right way, and sent his lover over the edge of restraint and into the depths of coital bliss.

The sight of Aric's chest rising and falling and the sound of his ragged breathing was enough to turn any man on, but to know Matt had driven him to that level of pleasure was the best ego stroking Matt could've asked for. It was enough to rouse an explosive orgasm, and as Matt pulled out of Aric's body and all that waving tightness rode over his shaft, Matt came again. He filled the condom to the brink of combustion and fell back on the floor, panting and listening to the rhythm of his racing pulse beating beneath his flesh.

They lay on the floor, fighting to breathe, fighting not to pass out right there. Matt rubbed his hand over his stomach and felt Aric's slick, warm release clinging to his skin.

"I hope you don't plan on running away immediately," Aric rasped.

"I couldn't move right now if I wanted to," Matt said, voice quivering with restrained laughter and lack of air.

"Good. I want to relish this feeling for a moment. I think that was the best lay I've had in a very long time."

"Glad you enjoyed my um… talent."

"Oh, 'enjoy' seems like such a harsh understatement."

CHAPTER THIRTEEN

THE SOUND of a phone blaring some horrible monophonic ringtone woke Matt from an incredible dream. Brandon was sitting on the bed behind him. Matt had his head in his lover's lap. They were comparing the rings they'd slid on each other's fingers a few days earlier, when they'd vowed to love each other and care for each other 'til death parted them.

What a horribly cruel dream, and the ringing from the phone was just as cruel for taking Brandon away from him again.

He lifted his head, and his neck cracked, sending a wave of pain down his spine and into his toes. It hurt like hell. He hadn't woken up that stiff in a long damn time. And when he gave up fighting to sit up for a moment, his head dropped back down, as if it hung loose from his shoulders. The back of his head hit something hard, hard enough to make a burst of stars erupt behind his eyelids. Matt ran his palm over whatever was beneath him and found the solid surface of a floor and the rough fibers of Berber. No wonder he'd woken up in a knotted ball of tense muscles. He'd spent an entire night curled in a ball on a hard floor.

He sat up, and his tailbone ground against the rough carpet. The phone rang again. Matt groaned as he scrubbed his hands over his face. He didn't remember falling asleep, only the amazing sex he'd had with Aric and the bittersweet dream he'd woken up from. This escape from Tennessee wasn't supposed to be about hooking up with random strangers and fucking his way to freedom from his past, but there he was, butt-naked with dried semen on his chest and a used condom on the floor beside him.

The phone rang again.

"You going to catch that?" Aric called from the direction of the kitchen.

Matt smelled bacon cooking, and maybe fresh bread or something similar. He heard footsteps pounding across the floor. Then Aric appeared in the doorway, half-clothed, holding a skillet and a spatula, and staring at Matt like he'd lost his mind.

"Your phone is ringing," he said.

"I know. It woke me up."

"Well, aren't you going to answer it?"

"Can I wake up first?"

"Sure. It's your phone." Aric frowned as he ducked back behind the wall again. He called out, "Does Mr. Grumpy need some coffee?"

Mr. Grumpy? Matt groaned again as he pushed up from the floor. He didn't have a stitch of clothing on and was only covered by a thin sheet. The fire from last night still crackled behind him and had to be the only reason he felt remotely warm.

He tightened the sheet around his torso, then headed into the kitchen. "Thanks for letting me fall asleep on the floor," he grumbled as he leaned against the counter and reached for a piece of buttered bread.

"I fell asleep right beside you, sweetheart. In fact, when I woke up, I found myself using you for a pillow."

"Coffee?"

"Right there," Aric nodded toward a black contraption sitting on the kitchen counter. Well, it sort of looked like a coffeemaker, but…. "It's a Keurig, Matt. It makes coffee by the cup."

"Okay, but how does it work?"

"Go, honey, clean up, and I'll get your coffee going."

"Thanks," Matt muttered, then turned and padded back out of the room.

He grabbed his pants from where they'd been piled in the floor, and his phone started ringing again. Whoever it was could wait until he'd had his coffee. He wasn't exactly in any sort of mood to pleasantly speak with anyone, but the phone didn't stop and wouldn't stop until he either answered it or turned it off.

The moment he lifted the stupid noisemaker from his pants pocket, he saw his brother's name on the screen. "Shit." His brother was probably freaking out right now. Matt never said anything about staying away all night, and he'd borrowed Mark's truck for this little adventure.

"Hello?" he said into the phone, voice still gravelly from just waking up.

"Where the hell are you? I've been calling you all damn morning!" Mark growled.

"Calm down. Calm down. I had a little too much wine last night and decided to crash at Aric's house."

"Jesus Christ, Matt! I've been freaking out for hours." He heard his brother sigh.

Matt cradled the phone between his ear and shoulder, hopping around on one foot as he struggled to get the wrinkled khakis he'd worn last night up his leg. "I'm fine, bro. I just didn't want to risk driving home."

"I wish you would've called me."

"Yeah, I would've, but I passed out on the floor."

"Sounds like you had more than a little wine."

Yeah, sure did, didn't it? He wasn't about to tell his older brother he'd passed out from exhaustion after a night of mind-blowing sex with a perfect stranger. Wouldn't that just make the situation a whole lot better?

"So," Mark said, "you heading home soon?"

"Soon. Yeah. Aric made breakfast. I probably need to hang around and eat since he went through the trouble."

"Damn, you already got the dude making you breakfast. Must've rocked his world," Mark teased. Matt slapped his palm against his forehead. He so wasn't going to have *that* conversation with his big brother. "I'm messing with you, man. Just get home when you can. It doesn't look like the storm is going to be as bad as they thought, and I want to get the season started. I could use the money, you know?"

"Yeah, I know. I'll be home soon, I swear."

"Cool."

"Later."

"Later."

Matt hung up the phone and set it down on the end table so he could fasten his pants, and when he swung around, Aric was standing behind him with a cup of coffee in one hand and a plate full of food in the other.

"Everything okay?" Aric asked.

"Yeah. It was my brother. He was concerned when he woke up and found I hadn't been home. He worries about me."

"Understandable." Aric handed over the cup of coffee and the plate of food he'd made. He said, "We can eat by the fire or at the kitchen table. I wasn't sure which you preferred."

"The table's good for me."

Aric nodded, then turned and headed for the kitchen. Matt followed. He took a seat at the table, and Aric joined him, handing over a fork as he sat down beside Matt.

They quietly ate their food—a warm helping of fluffy golden eggs and a few slivers of bacon, some fresh bread, and a tall a cup of some of the best coffee Matt had ever tasted. Matt polished off everything but the bacon. Pork was another no-no in their house. Brandon traded the pig he'd once loved so much for turkey, and it just wasn't the same.

"You don't eat bacon?" Aric asked.

"No. My ex took it out of my diet. Haven't had any in close to five years."

"God, I couldn't imagine. I love bacon. It's one of the best things about breakfast."

"Oh, I love it too, but—"

"So why don't you have some. It's not like he can tell you no anymore, right?"

"True." Matt shrugged, eyeing the brownish-red slivers of fried meat.

He could feel his mouth starting to water. Aric had a point. Brandon was no longer around to tell him no and to ostracize him for the choices he made in regards to the quality of food he ingested. He picked up one of the crispy slivers and stared at it for a moment, remembering how his mother had raised him and his brother on the greasy goodness, and they'd both turned out okay. Matt stuck the piece of meat in his mouth, and the moment it hit his tongue, he moaned.

He chewed and swallowed, took another bite, chewed and swallowed again. Aric watched him with a grin curling his delicious lips. "I can't believe I let Brandon take this away from me," he said after devouring one whole sliver. He went after the next piece with a new ferociousness.

"You look like you've only discovered bacon for the first time." Aric laughed.

"If you knew the orgasm my taste buds are having, you would understand."

Aric only laughed harder. "The look on your face is precious. It's like a small child tasting chocolate for the first time."

"Mmm… I had my first taste of chocolate last night," he teased.

Aric reached across the table and laid his hand on Matt's forearm. He brushed his thumb over the hard bone and smiled at Matt. "I hope you'll come back for more," he said. "I rather enjoyed myself."

All the chewing stopped. Matt reached for a napkin and wiped the grease from his hand. He turned in his chair to face Aric. The eager, blissful expression instantly fell away from Aric's face, as if he never expected the talk he was about to get.

"I don't know how long I'm going to be here," Matt finally said. "I mean, I had fun last night, and I would like to see you again, but… I can't get wrapped up in anything serious, ya know?"

"Oh, I'm not looking for anything serious either, as I said last night. I just enjoyed your company and wouldn't mind another night like we had. I haven't had sex like that in a long time. I think it did my body good."

"Okay, well, maybe when I come back, we can plan another date?"

"How long will you be gone?"

"A week, maybe longer. I'm not sure. I don't exactly know the ins and outs of lobster fishing. I suppose it'll depend on the weather and how well we're doing. I… I just don't know."

"It's okay. We'll figure it out," Aric offered. He let go of Matt's arm and sat back in his chair. "I have a few business trips planned over the next few weeks, but you can always call me. I wouldn't mind hearing from you."

"I think I can manage that."

"That would be nice."

Aric stood from the table and collected their empty plates. Matt went back into the living room and finished getting dressed. The sound of Aric washing dishes mingled with the crackling of the fire. Things suddenly felt very surreal, as if Matt had stepped out of some strange dream and only just now regained control of his body. It wasn't like him to have sex with someone he didn't know, and it wasn't like him to have awkward, next-day small talk over breakfast with the man he'd screwed the night before. Matt never did the casual-sex thing, and he didn't exactly know how to handle it. Aric seemed to be taking it well, as if he'd done this song and dance before—a thought that sort of bothered Matt.

"I'm about to go," Matt called from the living room sofa as he pulled his brother's shoes onto his feet. "I have to get back to my brother's house."

Aric appeared in the doorway, wiping his hands in a dishcloth. Even though Matt had told him he had to leave, Aric still had a smile on his face. "You'll be careful, right?"

"Of course." Matt stood and started across the living room. Aric met him halfway. "I'll call you when I get home, if you want me to."

"I would like that."

The draw he'd felt to Aric last night came back full force. He closed his eyes and parted his lips as he leaned in, hoping Aric would meet him for a good-bye kiss. Aric's warm, plump, kissable mouth pressed to his. The feel and taste made Matt step forward, made him wrap his arms around Aric's body and pull him into a hug. He pushed his tongue between the part in Aric's lips and the kiss deepened.

For a moment, Matt didn't want to let go. He didn't want to stop kissing Aric and didn't want to say good-bye. That scared the hell out of him. In no way, shape, or form was he ready to start heading down that path with anyone, let alone someone he'd just met and fucked. If he wanted to fall in love so easily, he would've been back home with Luke, exploring feelings he'd had for twenty years, not in New England running away from everything he'd ever known.

"I have to go," Matt said hoarsely as he released Aric's incredible lips.

"I know," Aric whispered with an unmistakable air of disappointment.

"I'll call you."

68

"You do that."

Matt's jaw tensed as he moved past Aric and headed out the side door. He felt bad for leaving the way he did, even though they'd had the talk long before they'd ever had sex. He felt even worse for even considering forgetting Aric existed after he'd promised to keep in touch. Matt just couldn't do the "getting attached to someone" thing right now. He wasn't ready to let someone have enough power to break his heart again. It was too soon, way too soon.

He unlocked Mark's truck and climbed behind the wheel, cranked the thing, and let his head rest against the seat as the engine warmed. He didn't plan on staying too long, not until his phone rang again and he saw Brandon's name on the screen.

"Shit!"

Chapter Fourteen

"I MISS you," Brandon said. Matt bit down so hard it felt like his teeth would explode under the pressure. He was doing a damn fine job of holding back the stream of curses he'd been saving up just for Brandon's ears. "What I did to you was wrong, but I thought it would take something extreme to make you see how much our relationship was killing me."

"Fuck you, Brandon," Matt said hoarsely. His voice quivered with anger and hurt and the myriad other things he felt in that moment, even the guilt of screwing someone when he was so clearly loved by someone else… or two someone elses for that matter. That four-letter swear wasn't just an homage to Brandon and the Dear John letter he'd left for Matt to find, but it was meant for Matt's conscience, which had started kicking his ass the moment he'd told Aric he had to go.

"I suppose I deserve that," Brandon said softly.

"You're damn right you do. Do you have any idea what you've put me through, what I've done because of you?"

"I heard your mom is selling the house. Where did you move to?"

"I left Tennessee for a while."

"What did you do with Zeus?"

"He's at Luke's house."

"Luke?" Brandon sounded genuinely astounded, like he had any damn nerve.

"Yeah, Luke. Got a problem with that?"

"Actually, I do. How could you leave our dog with him?"

"Our dog? Our fucking dog! You abandoned him. You abandoned us. So the way I see it, you have no claim over the dog, the house, me, or anything else. You left us."

Silence. He could hear Brandon's breathing and knew there were probably tears falling from Brandon's eyes. And even though his ex deserved to feel the pain and deserved to shed a few tears, Matt felt like shit for being so mean. He wasn't that guy. He wasn't the kind who held a grudge and cursed someone for leaving. He wasn't the guy who had one-night stands and left with uncaring good-byes. He wasn't the guy who ran away from everything because it was too much to deal with. Brandon turned him into that guy. Brandon made him that way, and he feared no amount of trying would turn him back into the man he once was.

"What did you want from me?" he said softly, clenching his jaw just as tight as before.

"I hoped—"

"What, Brandon? What did you hope? That you could call me and say you're sorry and I would come rushing back home? Did you think things could just go back to being the way they were?"

"I—"

"No. No. No. They can't. It doesn't work that way. I've never been so damn hurt before in my life. You broke my fucking heart, and you destroyed the trust I had for… for everyone, really. I can't just go back to being what we were. I can't marry you and start my life over with you."

"Marry me?" Brandon sounded confused.

"Yeah, marry you. I bought the rings six months ago. I'd planned on proposing. I was just waiting for the right time." Matt's voice grew significantly calmer than it had been. He could even hear the regret and pain that hadn't been there before. "I wanted to spend the rest of my life with you."

"I'm so sorry, Matt. I didn't know."

"You didn't want to know. You just wanted to escape."

"I didn't want to hurt you."

"Well, you sure picked a hell of a way of not hurting me."

"Matt…."

"You know what, Brandon, I have to go. I'm up north with my brother. I'll talk to you when I can."

He didn't give Brandon a chance to say another word. Matt hung up the phone and tossed it across the cab of his brother's truck. He was so mad, so pissed off he hadn't felt the stinging of tears in his eyes until he no longer had someone to yell at. He hadn't even felt those tears drip down his cheeks until he covered his face with his palms and growled out a string of curses.

When he finally removed his hands and opened his eyes again, through his watery gaze, he saw a wavering image of Aric standing a few feet from the truck. He had a frown on his face and worry in his stare, if not a hint of curiosity as well. Neither man immediately moved, as though neither one of them were sure how to react to Matt's private breakdown.

Matt left the keys dangling in the ignition as he climbed out of the cab. With hesitation in his step, he approached Aric, and his one-night lover did nothing more than hold out his arms. That's all Matt needed right now, someone to hold him while his ex's words trampled over his heart and mind. Matt's shoulders began to tremble as he stepped into Aric's embrace.

"Cry all you like," Aric whispered, pressing his lips to Matt's temple. "I won't judge."

Somehow, Matt knew that already. He felt safe and secure breaking down in Aric's arms, even though they'd just met. For some reason, he felt like he could let go and Aric wouldn't consider him weak.

In a tear-filled voice, Matt said, "Why did he have to call me? I was doing fine, and he had to call, and…."

"Some people don't realize how badly they've hurt someone, and they don't think before opening their damn mouths."

Matt felt Aric's warm, strong hand brushing up and down the center of his back, and he closed his eyes as he tightened his hold on Aric's body. He held the other man like that until Matt felt pretty certain all the tears had fled from his eyes and he could now face the long drive back to his brother's home alone.

He lifted his head from Aric's shoulder and pressed their foreheads together. Their lips were mere inches apart, and though he wanted to kiss Aric for giving him the support he needed when he needed it, he didn't do it. Now just didn't feel like the right time, not with his ex-partner on his mind and his one-night stand in his arms.

Now felt like the right time to flee for his life before he gave another man the power to break his heart.

"You okay?" Aric asked.

Matt nodded. "I think I'll be fine to drive now."

"Please be careful, and if the quiet gets to be too much, call me. Promise?"

"I promise. Thank you for letting me cry on your shoulder. I feel like such a dolt."

"Don't, okay? If you ever need a shoulder, you know where to find me."

"I do."

Aric pressed a chaste kiss to Matt's cheek, then released him from the hug. They kept their eyes locked on each other, even as Matt backed away. There was now something that looked like genuine sorrow in Aric's dark brown stare, something that looked like a mix of sympathy and pity. Matt hated the idea of anyone having pity on him. He wasn't the kind of guy who needed or wanted people feeling sorry for him, and he detested the fact he'd found himself in that position, especially with someone he was attracted to.

He backed out of Aric's driveway, following the GPS built into the dash as it guided him back to the highway. The quiet inside the cab of his brother's Denali became smothering and almost dizzying. If Matt let his mind continue to simmer in Brandon's words, he knew he would go insane fast, but nothing on the radio offered any comfort. It was all talk radio and power ballads or all that poppy crap the boys in the gay clubs loved so much but Matt couldn't stand. He looked over at the phone on the passenger seat only briefly, long enough to consider calling someone who could take his mind off Brandon.

Mark was out of the question. He loved his brother, but they weren't close enough to discuss Matt's love life. Not anymore. He loved his mother, but she wasn't the best listener. She often got angry when there was really no need to. He sure the hell wouldn't call Aric, because wouldn't that make him look incredibly desperate, even though Aric had offered to listen? The only person Matt really had left was Luke, and he presented a whole new set of problems.

And of those few people, Luke was the only one he had any real desire to confide in.

He reached across the console and blindly searched for the phone, keeping his stare glued to the road so he wouldn't wreck his brother's ride. His hand hit the phone, and he swiped it from the seat. He cautiously scrolled through the list of contacts until he reached Luke's name. For some reason, though, he couldn't make himself hit the call button.

CHAPTER FIFTEEN

MATT WHITE-KNUCKLED his phone all the way back to his brother's house on the upper east side of Connecticut. That little nerve-wrecker was the only life support he had right now. As long as he kept holding it, he could ride out the stormy waters of his life and not drown. As long as he held the phone in his hand and argued with himself, he wouldn't call Luke and he wouldn't call Aric and he….

"I'm losing my mind."

And that's exactly why he couldn't wait to get out to sea and make himself busy with the business of catching lobster with his big brother. There wouldn't be any time to lament over lost loves and bad decisions, or kisses that should've never happened. The sea was dangerous, and he wouldn't have any choice but to stay focused on work and keeping himself alive. And that's the whole reason he'd started this adventure in the first place, not to find someone new and not to harp on what he left behind in Tennessee.

Pulling into his brother's driveway, the feeling of being "home" again settled his mind. If nothing else, having Mark to hang out with would keep his head off the guys in his life. Or at least, that was the hope. If he knew Mark, his brother would have their bags packed and ready to head back to New Hampshire.

He parked the Denali in front of the garage, didn't bother locking it, then headed into the house. He heard Mark's voice before he saw his brother's long-legged form stretched out on the couch with the phone to his ear.

"Yeah, I think I just heard Matt come in. We'll head that way soon." Mark paused as if the person on the other end was saying something to him. "Yeah, I'll be safe, babe. No worries. See you soon."

As Mark hung up the phone, he turned his sun-bleached head back and glanced over the arm of the sofa. "Hey, man."

"Hey," Matt said flatly as he pitched the keys to the Denali onto the coffee table. He sat down on a chair next to the couch where his brother lay. "So we headin' out now?"

"Yeah. I was waiting for you to get back with the truck."

"Well, I'm back."

"I see." Mark frowned as he sat up. He kept his stare on Matt. "You okay?"

"I will be."

"Wanna talk about it?"

"Not really."

"Fair enough. Let me grab my things and we'll roll."

"Mind if I change first?"

"Sure, I left a pile of clothes in your room, just some stuff that'll work for you on the boat. You can leave your dirties on the bed. Emma's going to come up and clean the house while we're gone."

"That's nice of her."

"Yeah," Mark said a bit airily. He had that hooded, hopelessly in love, goofy daze in his eyes. He seemed to get that every time he talked about Emma, even though Mark kept trying to play their relationship off as nothing serious. "She likes taking care of me."

"Sounds like a keeper."

"Maybe." Mark shrugged, standing up from the couch. He swiped a T-shirt from the armrest and pulled it over his head, then all the way down past the waist of his jeans. "I'm going to throw my shit in the truck. Get movin', okay?"

"Moving. Gotcha. You think I have time for a shower?"

"Can you take one at Emma's place?"

He looked down at his covered stomach and remembered what he and Aric did last night. Really, he *needed* a shower—a nice long soak under some piping hot water. What he would take, if he couldn't have more, was a wet washcloth and some soap.

"Can I at least freshen up a little? I haven't had a shower since yesterday."

"So that's what I smell?" Mark smirked. Matt flipped him the bird. His brother laughed and said, "I'm kidding, man. Go ahead. Just hurry. I want to get to the boat before the rest of the crew does."

"Hurry. Gotcha."

Mark headed one way. Matt headed in the opposite direction, down the hall and back into the room he'd spent only one night in. Just as Mark promised, a stack of jeans and shirts were piled onto the bed, all neatly folded and ready to be packed into a bag. He grabbed his duffel bag from the chaise in the corner and dumped the dirties out, then carried it over to the bed and packed up the fresh clothes, all but one pair of jeans and a long-sleeved T-shirt so he could clean up and change. Luckily, he'd packed about five pair of boxer briefs because he didn't know when he would be able to buy more, but that didn't leave a whole lot of room for a bunch of changes of clothes.

He carried everything over to the bathroom and set it down on the edge of the vanity, then began to strip out of the nicer clothes he'd worn last night. The remnants of his evening with Aric still clung to Matt's tanned skin. It was a testament to a decision Matt probably should've made a little more carefully. Had he not been under the influence of wine and a very, very sexy man, he might've opted to drive on back to his brother's house. Sure, part of him might've needed a quick lay, but now he felt guilty, like he'd wronged Luke and wronged Brandon, though Brandon didn't really deserve a second thought.

He knelt down and reached in the vanity for a washcloth, stood, tossed it in the sink, and cranked up the hot water. The light blue cloth slowly grew darker as the water soaked through its fibers. He grabbed a bright green bar of soap and tossed it under the spray as well.

"Fresh as an Irish spring," he quipped as he rolled the bar around in his hand.

After squeezing off the excess water, he rubbed the soapy rag over his naked chest, scrubbing hard over the faint trail of deep brown curls dancing down his abdomen. He watched as the soap foamed in the coarse patch of hairs at the base of his shaft. He dragged the rag over his sac and back again. Then he rinsed the rag and repeated the process sans soapy film. It wasn't a shower, but at least he felt a little cleaner, less whorish… in a way.

He reached back under the counter and grabbed a plush blue towel, dried himself off, then doused himself in cologne and matching body spray, slicked his armpits with some deodorant, and proceeded to get dressed.

His brother's jeans were a little too loose for his taste, but it was something clean to cover his body with. The navy-blue long-sleeved T-shirt felt like a tent on him, but again, something clean, and he wouldn't complain. He had fresh socks and underwear, and frankly, he was ready to have the weight of his heavy steel-toed boots on his feet again. They made him feel grounded, which he really needed right now, because he felt like he'd been aimlessly floating through his life for the last two weeks. He ran a brush through his long brown hair, enough to get rid of the tangles and nothing more, then packed his toiletries away in their bag before heading back over to his room to grab the rest of his things.

With his duffel bag in hand, Matt headed out to the Denali to join his brother. The next three hours would be spent in the car, hopefully not talking about love lives and where things went wrong, hopefully not dwelling on relationships and things that might've been avoided had communication actually occurred before the Dear John letter was signed.

"You ready, little bro?" Mark called from the other side of the truck.

Matt walked around to join him. "As ready as I'll ever be, I guess," he said as he handed Mark his bag.

"Everything'll be all right. The crew's gonna love you, man."

"Hey," Matt said, grabbing Mark's forearm to get his attention. He didn't want the seriousness of the question he was about to ask to be lost on his slightly aloof-at-times older brother. "Does your crew know about me?"

"What about you?"

"That I'm gay?"

"No. I didn't tell 'em. It's not any of their damn business. Why?"

"Just wanted to know what I was getting into. Some guys don't like having to change their clothes or bunk anywhere near the gay guy."

"Honestly, bro, I don't think anyone on my crew is that narrow-minded, but if keeping that tidbit to yourself makes you feel better, go right ahead."

"Thanks, man. It does make me feel better."

CHAPTER SIXTEEN

BACK IN New Hampshire, Matt's nerves had finally started to settle a little, partly thanks to the overwhelming welcoming hugs he'd gotten from his brother's girlfriend, partly because there was now just over a hundred fifty miles of land between him and the bad decision he'd made last night. Not that he saw anything wrong with Aric, only that he wasn't ready to get involved in any way with another person. Not yet.

Mark and Emma were into some pretty heavy conversation from the looks of it, and Mark's crew had yet to arrive. That gave Matt some time to make a few phone calls and check on his precious Harley, which had been left in a locked garage for two days. He'd grabbed the keys from Emma before the conversation had gotten too deep, and he took off out into the cool fall New Hampshire afternoon, back toward the garage where he'd left his baby.

Once he found himself well away from the locals and hidden back where no one could accidentally get an earful, he pulled out his phone and searched through his contacts until he found Luke's number again.

The last time he'd talked to Luke, things hadn't gone so well, and Matt had a nagging feeling he really needed to make everything right with his best friend before heading out into the dangerous ocean. If something happened to either of them before he had a chance to talk things out with the person closest to him, he would never be able to forgive himself, and the thought of missing his chance would end up pinging around in his head until it made him crazy.

This time, he pushed the call button and patiently waited for Luke to answer.

"Didn't think I would be hearing from you," Luke said.

"I couldn't go out on the boat without talking to you first."

"Well, I'm glad you called. I—"

"Luke, can you give me a minute. I have something I need to get off my chest before you say anything."

Silence. He could almost picture Luke stomping back and forth as he paced the short length of his Midtown Memphis living room. Matt thought he heard the slapping of bare feet and the creaking of hardwood.

"Luke?"

"Go ahead."

"I didn't leave Memphis because I wanted to. I left because I had to. I couldn't stop thinking about Brandon. I still haven't stopped thinking about Brandon... or you for that matter. The kiss threw me, so much so I didn't stop and think about what I was doing when I kissed you back. I didn't stop to consider what was going on in your head, if maybe you'd always felt the same way I did. We've never discussed sexuality, and I always thought you were straight. If I would've known...."

"Matt, I was too afraid to let anyone know. You know how my family is. They're all a bunch of self-righteous homophobes. I thought, or... or rather, I hoped that if I just ignored the way I felt, it would go away. When I met you and we bonded so fast, I thought I finally had someone I could be myself with, but I was still so damn afraid of going after what I wanted."

"You've always wanted me too?" Matt asked as he leaned against the side of the garage. He needed something solid to help hold him up, because it felt like the world was sinking around him.

"Yeah, I have," Luke admitted.

"Jesus. Christ."

"Yeah."

"I slept with someone last night."

Again, the line fell silent. He wasn't sure why he'd told Luke about his bad decision. For some silly reason, it felt like the right thing to do, like he owed Luke the honesty. Or maybe he just needed to say it out loud, and Luke had been the only unfortunate soul he felt like he could talk to about it.

"Luke?"

"I'm still here."

"I'm sorry."

"What are you apologizing for? You don't owe me anything. We're not together."

"I needed to. I feel like I owe you a hell of a lot. I feel like if I would've told you about how I felt a long time ago, things would've turned out very different for both of us." Matt sighed as he pushed back up from the wall. He started to pace a tight circle. "I don't know why I slept with Aric. He was there, and I was lonely. I wanted to stop hurting. But it didn't make the pain go away. Sleeping with him only made it worse."

"Do you have feelings for him?" Luke quietly asked.

"No," Matt blurted. "No, I don't. Neither one of us were looking for anything involved. It was just sex."

"Matt, not for nothing, but where is this conversation going?"

"I don't know. I just wanted to apologize to you before we headed out. If something happened to me on the boat—"

"Stop, okay? Don't talk like that."

"I have to. I'm being realistic." Matt swallowed hard as he ran his shaking hand through his hair. "If something happened to me, I didn't want the last words we said to each other to be angry. I wanted… just to let you know I was sorry."

"When are you coming home?"

"I don't know."

"Matt, if you're really sorry and you want to make things up to me, then go out to sea and get that out of your system. Do whatever you have to do to get over Brandon, then come back home. You can stay with me if you want to. Just please, come back home."

"Plan on it, okay? It might be a few weeks or so, but plan on it."

"Zeus will be happy to have his daddy back."

Whether it was what Luke said or how he said it, Matt didn't know, but he suddenly felt his throat tightening and his eyes burning, as if he were trying to fight tears he didn't know he had. Those wretched wet droplets hitting his cheek made him want to yell out a string of curses, and he swore to God if his brother hadn't been counting on him to man the boat this season, he would've jumped on his bike and headed back west to Tennessee, just so he could be where he truly belonged.

It took a minute and few failed attempts to clear his throat before he trusted his voice enough to say, "You be careful. I'll call you as soon as I'm on land again."

"You take care too. I'll be looking forward to hearing your voice again."

The call ended, and Matt pressed the phone to his sternum as he sank down where he stood. His ass planted on the concrete floor of the garage, and he pulled his knees up to his chest. He just needed a minute, one minute… maybe two. If he was going to play all manly in front of his brother's crew, Matt knew he needed to shed a few tears and get over it before he faced anyone else.

It was the sound of Emma's voice calling his name that finally made him snap out of his melancholy. The door to the garage opened, and bright gray light spilled into the faintly lit room. He quickly brushed his hand over his cheeks, hoping the glistening tracks of his shed tears would be completely wiped away before Emma had a chance to notice them.

She asked, "Why are you sitting in the middle of the floor," to which Matt said nothing but immediately bounded to his feet.

"I had a few calls to make." *Well one, but who's counting?*

"Your brother told me to come get you. Said the crew's here, and they're ready to start boarding the boat."

"Thanks," Matt said as he urgently started past her, but she stopped him by grabbing his arm.

She eyed him for a long moment—brows creasing, steely blue eyes piercing through to his soul, lips pursed. He had the urge to squirm, like a child who'd just gotten caught doing something he wasn't supposed to be doing. She tilted her head and asked, "What's wrong?"

"Nothing," he quickly responded, immediately averting his eyes.

"Look. I don't know what the deal is with you Murphy boys, but you guys make the worst liars ever. So come on now, what's going on."

"I made a mistake," Matt said, hoping to get her off his back, but the woman seemed to be just as stubborn as their mother. She didn't let go and didn't look away, and Matt would've sworn he was staring into the scrutinizing stare of his beloved mom. "I hid my feelings from someone important to me, and had I just owned up to what I felt, things would've turned out very differently. But I didn't, and now I have to make it right."

"Sweetheart," she said softly, and Matt immediately looked up. Her stare transformed from piercing and demanding to soft and sincere. "Admitting you made a mistake is the first step to making things right again. Now you just have to follow through. Hear me?"

"Loud and clear."

"Good." Emma gave him a quick pat on the shoulder and a genuine smile. "Now go out there and be safe. I'm sure that special someone wants to see you make it home."

He gave Emma a crooked grin, then headed back out into the cold afternoon. Mark stood at the edge of the docks with Matt's duffel bag at his feet. Behind him were two mammoth men, significantly larger than Mark, decked out in bright yellow suits that looked like rain slicks. Huge galoshes covered their legs up to their knees. They both had on bright orange toboggans, and their five-o'clock shadows left a hell of a lot to be desired. At least Matt didn't find either of them attractive. Nothing to be worried about in *that* department.

"Guys," Mark said, "this is my little brother, Matt. Matty, meet the crew."

CHAPTER SEVENTEEN

THE BIG guy who'd been on Mark's left—Scotty they called him, not because it was his name, but because he was actually Scottish, and the nickname stuck from day one—was the one in charge of showing Matt the ropes. That sucked royally for Matt since he could barely understand a word Scotty said.

He tossed Matt a pile of the same bright yellow outfits they were wearing and told him to head down into the belly of the boat to change. They planned on pulling anchor in about twenty minutes, and if Matt wanted to have a chance in hell of staying dry, he'd better get a move on it.

Matt's steel-toed boots thumped and thudded against the metal stairs as he stomped his way down to the cabin of the boat. His brother sat on one of the couches with a cell phone pressed to his ear. "I know, Ma," he said. "Matty'll be fine. I won't let nothin' happen to him. I promise." Mark paused. "Yeah, I'll call you as soon as we get back. Stop worrying about him, okay? I've done this before, and I know how to run a safe ship."

Matt could almost hear his mother from clear across the room. She had that begging lilt with the cold hardness of being a strict mother. There was no telling how long she'd been chewing Mark's ear off about taking care of Matt.

"Give me the phone," Matt said with undeniable authority, so much authority his brother quirked his brow and stared up at Matt as if he'd somehow sprouted a second head. "Let me talk to her."

"Hang on, Mom," Mark said as he held the phone up for Matt.

Matt all but snatched it from his brother's hand. "Mom, it's Matt."

"I thought you were going to call me!" she exclaimed.

"Things came up. Now, stop worrying Mark, please. He's going to get everyone home safe and sound, okay? But he can't get this boat launched if he's on the phone with you."

"I know, Matty, I just—"

"Mom. Please."

"Fine. Whatever. Call me the moment you get back to dry land, or I'll worry about you."

"I know. Hey, Mom?"

"Yeah?"

"Don't put the house up for sale just yet, okay?" And before she could launch into an interrogation about why he didn't want to sell the house and if he was coming back, Matt said, "I love you. Gotta go," then ended the call.

"Smart move," Mark said. "Now, why don't you want her selling the house? I thought you were ready to move on."

Matt sat down beside his brother and unfolded the plastic yellow pants Scotty had given him. He held them down at his feet and dipped each foot inside the respective leg, then hoisted the heavy suit up his body.

"When you sent Emma looking for me, I was in the garage talking to Luke," Matt admitted without looking his brother in the eyes.

"Luke Bishop?" Mark asked.

Matt caught a glimpse of his brother's slack jaw and agape mouth from the corner of his eye. Why the hell that surprised Mark was anyone's guess. Luke and Matt had never kept their friendship a secret from anyone, and it was also no big secret that they'd stayed in touch throughout the years. But Matt had forgotten how long it had been since he'd really talked to his brother on any level.

"Yeah, Luke Bishop," Matt finally said.

"You two still talk?"

"Of course. We're best friends."

"Hell, I didn't know." Mark pressed his palms to the air. "Calm down, bro, I was just asking."

"I know, but...." Matt shook his head and sighed. "There's more to it."

"Need to talk about it?"

"I don't think so. No offense, but I'm not talking about my personal life with you."

"Why not? I'd share mine with you."

"Do you really want to hear about me being in love with another man, Mark?"

"You're in love with Luke Bishop? Does he know?" Mark looked and sounded genuinely shocked. Made sense, especially since no one had known about Luke's sexuality... including Matt.

"You really want to hear this, don't you?"

"I asked, didn't I?"

With a sigh, Matt sat back on the bench seat and rubbed his hands over his face. He thought long and hard about exactly what he would tell Mark about the situation with Luke, how much detail he would give his very straight brother who'd once been married to the most homophobic bitch under the stars. He spared the details of the kiss, but laid the rest of it out for Mark to devour. He told his brother about how they'd both hidden their feelings and now that there was so much distance between them, they only wanted to be close to each other again. Mark asked about the guy from last night, and Matt told him that Aric was just a lay, that really and truly his heart belonged to Luke—always had and always would. Mark seemed to be very understanding. "So that's why I told Mom not to sell the house."

"Wow."

"That's all you have to say?"

"Well, that's a lot of information to take in. I um—" Mark lowered his head a little, and with it, his voice grew quieter. "—thought you would want to stay up here, especially if I convinced Mom to move up this way."

Okay, sure, Matt had considered it for like... a split second, but Tennessee was home, always had been and always would be. Besides, Luke was in Tennessee, and at the moment, Matt wanted to be as close to his longtime friend as he could get, and if that meant going back to Memphis and staying there, then that's where he would go.

"Mark...."

"Don't, man. You don't have to explain anything. You don't have to say anything. I get it. Really. I do. You have to go wherever you're going to be happy. I wouldn't expect anything less, you hear me?"

"Yeah, man. I hear you."

They immediately stood up, but Mark was first to wrap his arms around Matt's body. Matt took a deep breath and slowly let it go. Admittedly, it felt damn good to have his brother back again, to be as close as they had been growing up. He closed his eyes for a moment, only a few short minutes, and Mark whispered against his ear. "I love you, man. I always have. Don't forget that, okay?"

"I won't. I promise," Matt said in an equally airy voice.

CHAPTER EIGHTEEN

THE WEIGHT of all that damn protective gear made Matt feel like he was lugging around an extra fifty or so pounds. He was used to carrying a utility belt around a job site, but all those layers of clothes seemed a bit excessive... until they got out on the water, in the freezing spray of the North Atlantic Ocean.

"Eh, Greenhorn," Scotty yelled, pointing across the main deck of the boat toward a stack of metal mesh and cage. "Toss me dem pots, wouldya? We needta get 'em packed with bait and ready for the first trawl."

Bait? Jesus Christ, Matt was doing good to stand on his wobbly legs without hurling all over the deck. Now these clowns expected him to play with bait? Had they lost their minds?

He gripped the rail and reached for the first pot. It was a hell of a lot heavier than it looked, and apparently it was tangled up with the other cages. Matt had no choice but to let go of the rail... unless he wanted to look like an ass who couldn't hack it.

Planting his feet a good twenty inches apart from each other, he kept his knees bent and carefully let go of the rail. The ocean churned. The waves reached up and drenched the three of them, nearly pulling Matt's legs out from under him. He quickly two-fisted the rail, and the rest of the crew started to laugh. He playfully flipped them both the bird, which only made them laugh harder.

"Eh, Greenhorn, you're lookin' a bit green in the gills dere," Scotty teased.

"Did I mention to you guys this is the first time I've ever been on a boat?"

Their laughter turned riotous.

"Thanks, guys. Real nice of you to help the new guy out."

That playing around—according to Mark—meant the guys liked him, which was a damn good thing considering they were all going to be stuck on that boat together for the next five days, maybe even longer if the pots came back light… whatever that meant.

"Go help him, you ass," the quiet guy said as he nudged the Scotsman toward Matt. "I wanna get off this damn boat before my kids have grandkids."

Chuckles shook his head full of bright copper hair, and he pounded his big ass across the boat. He reached one thick, meaty hand out and gripped Matt's shoulder hard enough to shock him out of his near nausea. It snapped Matt back so hard he felt like he could finally stand on his legs without falling over.

"Here, lad, take one of these," Scotty whispered, holding out his hand. He uncurled his fingers and in the palm of his hand was a little round white pill.

Matt frowned. He normally didn't take any kind of drugs. "What the hell is that?"

"Dramamine. It's for motion sickness. You can get it at any pharmacy, I promise."

"It's safe?"

"Of course, lad. I wouldn't give it ya if it weren't."

Matt swiped the pill from Scotty's hand and immediately popped it in his mouth before another wave could come along and wash it away. He swallowed it down with nothing to chase the pill from his throat. "Thanks," he mumbled.

"S'okay, Greenhorn. We've all been there, even your wee brother."

"Wee brother?" Matt arched his brow.

"Well, he is a tad tiny, yeah?"

"He's bigger than me."

"True. Now, grab dem pots and let's be gettin' a move on, yeah?"

Matt grabbed the first pot and slid it down the deck to Scotty. He held it steady while the quiet one shoved bait in the trap. They yelled for the next one, and Matt repeated the routine. He kept going until all twenty pots on the first trawl were lined up and set with bait. The bullhorn sounded, and Scotty lowered the gate at the boat's stern. He gave the first pot a shove, and it slid across the deck, then splashed into the ocean, pulling the other pots along with it.

The whole thing worked like a well-oiled machine. Matt could honestly admit how impressed he was that his brother could not only put something so incredible together, but seemed to be doing a good job keeping it running.

The last pot slid into the water, and something Scotty called a "high-flyer" tagged the beginning of the line. Matt looked back up to Scotty and said, "Now what?"

"Well, lad, we got five more trawls to set today. Then we can rest for a wee bit."

"Rest sounds great," Matt said.

"Enjoy it now," the quiet one said. "Once we pull the trawls from today, it's nothin' but back-breakin' labor from there."

"Great," Matt said flatly. Scotty laughed and shook his head. Matt was quickly beginning to realize the jollier of the two was the gentle giant with hair the color of a copper penny and bright freckles dotting his chubby cheeks. Those cheeks shined every time Scotty smiled wide, and God if his cheeky grin wasn't completely contagious.

They finished setting the remaining trawls, and the boat slowed to nothing more than an easy coasting, even though it still flopped around in the water. It wasn't as bad as it had been. The swell had died down, and it appeared Matt's first day on the boat was coming to an end.

"The Greenhorn making dinner tonight?" Mark asked as he hopped down from the wheelhouse.

"Dinner? Me? You're kidding, right?"

"Greenhorns always make dinner the first night, lad," Scotty said.

Matt arched a brow at his brother, who was now fighting damn hard not to burst into hysterical laughter. Matt could tell by the jostling of Mark's shoulders and the crow's feet in the corners of his eyes and the pale pressure lines around Mark's mouth as he pinched his lips together.

"Please tell me this is a joke," Matt said.

The quiet one shook his head.

"You guys really have no idea what you're getting yourselves into."

"Oh, I have an idea," Mark teased.

"Okay. Fine." Matt nodded a little too convulsively. "I'll make dinner."

They didn't know it, but Matt's idea of "making dinner" usually involved a cardboard box slung into the microwave or some brand of meat tossed between two slices of bread with a side of potato chips. The joke would be on them.

He headed down into the cabin, buried within the boat's hull, kicked off his galoshes, and left them in a tiny closet by the door. Then he shrugged out of the huge, yellow rain-slicking jacket and hung it on the peg beneath the piece of white tape with his name scribbled on it in black marker. He unclipped the suspenders holding up the heavy, matching yellow pants and hung them over his jacket.

Thankfully, the clothes beneath were as dry as when he'd put them on—a miracle considering the amount of water he'd been sloshing around in all day. It felt good to finally be out of all that gear, to have all that weight off his body.

He went straight to the kitchen—or rather, the "galley" as Mark had called it during the grand tour—and started digging through the few cabinets. He found loaves of wheat bread and a huge jar of peanut butter. There was no jelly to be found, but a whole stack of ripe, yellow bananas… and two family-sized bags of Doritos.

"Dinner is served," he said with a hint of laughter.

He grabbed four paper plates from the cupboard and sat them all out on the counter in a nice, tight row. Then he slapped four pieces of bread on each plate. Men that big obviously needed more than one sandwich. He slathered on the crunchy peanut butter, then took to peeling and slicing the bananas. By the time the guys got down there, their plates were set out nice and neat on the table, and Matt stood there with a winning grin on his face. "You wanted dinner. I made dinner."

"Jesus, Greenhorn, how the hell are we supposed to live off that?" the quiet one asked, pointing his thick meaty finger at the stacks of banana and peanut butter sandwiches.

"Would you rather me waste food *trying* to cook or risk food poisoning from my cooking?"

"It can't be that bad," Scotty offered.

In unison, both Matt and Mark said, "It's that bad."

CHAPTER NINETEEN

THE MOST grueling of the work came right after they'd pulled the first trawl back. Everything moved along at lightning speed. They pulled the traps, cleared out the lobsters and the abundance of soft-shell crabs, filled the traps with bait again, and readied them to go back into the ocean.

Apparently they did really well that first day, even with the eggers—the pregnant lobsters—and the puny ones they'd had to throw back. Mark was the happiest Matt had seen him since he'd arrived in New England. From the sounds of it, if the season kept up the way it was going, Mark would find himself back in the black again.

They were well into the fourth day at sea. It was a cold fall Thursday morning. The sun hadn't even begun to ascend on the horizon. The guys had all polished off a massive helping of bacon and eggs that the quiet guy—who still hadn't said his name—had made. It was probably the most satisfying meal Matt had ever eaten. They all made their way back up to the deck. Mark went straight to the wheelhouse to make sure the autopilot had kept them on course overnight.

The winds were a bit colder and much stronger than they had been during the previous days. It was so intense it felt like little needles prickling at Matt's cheeks. The ocean flopped the boat around a little more furiously than before, but Matt's stomach and legs remained on course thanks to Dramamine and a huge Scotsman.

The boat pitched hard to the left, and Matt grabbed the rail so he wouldn't be tossed across the deck. It made his heart jump in his chest.

"Scotty!" Mark called from the wheelhouse. There was a new urgency in his voice and concern in the way he looked past everyone to Scotty. "They've issued a gale warning."

"Got it, Skipper."

"What's a gale warning?" Matt yelled over the sound of waves crashing against the boat's hull. No one answered him.

The other two crew members immediately took to tying down cages. They moved with speed and focus, like they'd done this job a million times and "gale warnings" were nothing to worry about, just something to prepare for. Another day in the life of a lobsterman.

Matt felt completely helpless, standing there clueless but concerned. "What can I do?" he yelled again.

"Go fetch the tarp, lad. It's folded in the corner of the engine room," Scotty commanded.

As carefully but as fast as he could, Matt headed back down into the cabin, past the closet and the bunks, past the table and the galley, and straight back to the door he remembered Mark telling him led to the engine room. The handle jiggled, but the door didn't want to open, not easily. He bumped it with his hip, tugged, kicked, then bumped it again, and the door finally sprang free.

The smell of used motor oil and some brand of fuel stung his nostrils. He did his best not to breathe in the fumes and went straight over to the first corner where Scotty promised the tarp would be. Its shiny blue surface was like a beacon in the dirty, dim light.

He grabbed the tarp and tucked it under his arm, then started back toward the door. When he took the first step away from the engine, the boat pitched hard to the right, like it'd been slammed with a wave the size of a mountain. The force knocked Matt right off his feet, and the entire side of his body hit the metal wall hard enough he bounced back and dropped to his ass on the rough floor. A stream of four-lettered curses left his mouth in a winded rush. Pain shot up his arm and radiated down his back, all the way to his tailbone and down his legs.

Wincing, Matt rolled over onto his knees and pushed up onto all fours. He reached out for that tarp, then tucked it under his arm. The boat continued to rock—back and forth, back and forth. He didn't trust his legs to hold him up, to keep him from careening face-first into a wall or toppling down the stairs as he climbed his way back up to the deck. And God help him, the Dramamine was starting to wear off.

Somehow he managed to get back through the cabin and almost up to the deck. He stood on the steps, hanging from the doorknob and swaying with the boat. The door flapped with the raging wind, threatening to dump Matt down to the cabin's floor.

"Scotty!" he yelled from the top of the steps. The Scotsman raised his head. "Give me a hand, would ya?"

"I gotta tie down this pot, lad. Give me a—"

Before Scotty was able to finish his sentence, another wave crashed against the stern of the boat. The gate in the back had been left down because they'd been getting ready for another trawl, and the moment Matt saw the wave crest against the deck, he knew his new pal was in some serious trouble.

"Scotty!" Matt yelled, even as the water rolled over his body and down into the cabin.

It pulled him back down the steps and away from the door, just like a tide washing away sand beneath feet, as if he were standing at an ocean shoreline. It pulled him back into the cabin, dragging him along the rough edge of the metal steps.

Despite the pain in his limbs and back, Matt fought his way back up the steps and managed to reach the deck. He somehow made it to his feet and had the fortitude to storm forward. The quiet guy had one hand on the guard rail and one hand locked around Scotty. They were both fighting to pull Scotty back up but didn't have the power.

Matt grabbed one of the ropes that had been tied to the side of the boat and wrapped it around his wrist three times, held on, and eased his way to the edge of the boat, just like he would've done if he was working on a roof and had to lower himself down to the edge. He held out his free arm and hooked it around Scotty. Together, the two of them managed to pull the gentle giant back onto the boat.

"Hang on, man," Matt said. "Just hang on to us until this crap passes."

"I think I can kick up the gate," Scotty said, reaching his boot-covered foot toward the thick hunk of metal lying on the deck's floor. "I can get it. Just give me a few more inches."

"Don't do it," the quiet guy said. "You're pulling us down with you."

"Just a few more inches." Scotty kept struggling. The last reach nearly pulled him away from Matt's hold.

"Scotty!" Matt and the quiet man yelled in unison. "Stop."

But it was too late. Their hold on Scotty slipped, and he went tumbling back down toward the open-ended stern.

CHAPTER TWENTY

"YOU'RE INSANE. In-freaking-sane," Matt said as he rubbed his shoulder. "And you don't listen for shit."

"Ay, why in the hell would I listen to a greenhorn?" Scotty retorted.

"Hey, that greenhorn saved your ass," the quiet guy said.

"Suck it, Chuck," Scotty said as he gave his crotch a quick jerk.

They were all sitting against the now closed metal gate. Matt didn't want to move... ever again. That last brush with death would've been enough to scare the shit out of anyone. Scotty had been right, though. A few more inches, and he had the damn thing shut and secured before the swell ripped them all away from the boat.

"Your name is Chuck?" Matt asked after a long moment of silence, surprised he'd finally learned the quiet guy's name.

"One 'Chucky' joke and I'll kick your ass," Chuck said flatly.

Scotty laughed so hard his whole body shook.

Chuck gave him a droll stare.

Matt just closed his eyes and tried to relax for a minute, tried to listen for the beating of his heart. It'd been racing so hard it made his head pound. The adrenaline rush, combined with motion sickness threatened to make him hurl in Scotty's lap, but at least the storm was finally starting to calm.

"You guys okay?" Mark said as he climbed out of the wheelhouse.

"Yeah, the dumb guy and your baby brother almost swam with the fishies," Chuck said.

Mark gave Matt and Scott a *what-the-hell* look. They both shrugged.

It was more than clear the storm had worn out every one of them, even the skipper who'd spent the entire time trying to keep the boat on an even course. Thankfully, though, they'd caught a hell of a lot more crab and lobster than they'd expected to, so if Mark really wanted to, he could head back to dry land, rest for a week, then give it another go. He'd mentioned that plan to Matt when they'd arrived in New Hampshire almost a week ago. Best. Idea. Ever.

"So how waterlogged is the cabin?" Mark asked.

"Don't know," Matt said. "I was busy trying not to drown."

"I'll check it out," Scotty said.

"No." Mark pressed his palm to the air. "I got it. You guys just chill for a bit."

"I'm coming with you," Matt said as he pushed up from where he'd been sitting.

The ache hadn't left his bones yet, and as he stalked across the slick deck, he realized he'd developed a bit of a hobble. He eased down the stairs, careful not to fall on his ass again. No way could his tailbone take too many more hard falls.

The room wasn't nearly as flooded as he'd thought. Apparently, the grates in the steps and the drain underneath caught most of the water. A little had pooled on the tiles, but thankfully, most of the downstairs was dry. There weren't many surfaces made of water-absorbing fibers to begin with.

"Not too bad," Mark said, "We can take a pump to the few bad spots and everything'll be good as new." He looked back at Matt and frowned. "You're getting a bruise on your cheek. You okay?"

"I'm probably getting bruises everywhere." Matt shrugged. "Took a good tumble or two during all that mess."

"It happens."

"Yeah, I see."

"Hey, um… I saw how you helped Scotty out. Thanks for steppin' in the way you did."

"I couldn't let him just get dragged out to sea."

"I know. I know. Thing is, you didn't freeze in the face of danger. That's the kind of bravery a skipper needs on his boat. What do you think about doing this for me on a regular basis?"

"I don't know, man." Matt pulled the toboggan off his head and brushed back his wet hair. "I don't know if I'm cut out for this mess."

"You looked pretty cut out for it to me."

"Maybe, but I feel like a pounded lump of clay right now."

"You get used to it."

With an exaggerated sigh, Matt planted his ass on the bench. It felt good to sit down again, even if his tailbone felt like it had been smashed with a sledgehammer. He winced and shifted until he found a comfortable way to sit.

Coming back to New England and giving life at sea another chance just didn't sound like his idea of fun. Yeah, he wanted to help his big brother out, but some things were a little too dangerous, even for his taste. Besides, he had business to handle back in Memphis. Mark knew that. They'd discussed it once already.

When he looked back up at Mark, he found his brother's steely blue stare trained hard on him. It was the same look their dad used to give them both whenever they were supposed to be doing something they weren't, or even doing something they'd been told not to. It was a look that had once struck fear in the hearts of two boys who couldn't be separated no matter how hard someone tried to pry them apart.

"Mark," Matt said as he looked away again. "I can't do it, man. I have to go home and see if I can't work something out with Luke."

"Does Luke know about that night?"

"Yeah, I told him."

"How did Luke take it?"

"Okay, I guess. Why do you care?"

"I don't. I'm just askin'."

"Aric doesn't want anything serious," Matt said, and God did he hope Aric meant it when he'd said it. He hoped Aric wasn't just telling him what he wanted to hear to get Matt in the sack. If that was Aric's intention, boy, Matt sure was a sucker. "Yeah. No. Nothing serious."

"Who are you trying to convince, me or yourself?" Mark said, laughing under his breath.

Matt only glared.

"Guess that's my cue to leave well enough alone."

"Yes, it is," Matt said flatly.

Mark headed back up to the deck, leaving Matt alone again. Matt peeled the heavy yellow jacket away and threw it onto the other edge of the bench. He then slipped the suspenders that held up his slick pants down his arms and pulled his shirt over his head.

From the look of his sides and arms, he'd taken a pretty good beating and would probably end up sore as hell tomorrow. The right side of his body had already started turning purple. His entire right arm swelled a good bit. The sight alone was almost enough to zap what little energy he had left, and right then, he knew beyond a shadow of doubt, there was no way in hell he could do that kind of work on any sort of regular basis.

CHAPTER TWENTY-ONE

FRIDAY MARKED the very last day they had to spend on that damn boat. They'd caught almost seven hundred pounds of lobster and who the hell knew how much crab. At that point, Matt didn't care if he ever saw another crustacean again. What he did care about was the quickly approaching shoreline of Portsmouth and the fact that he'd get to sleep in a real bed again soon.

Murphy's Law had been the last boat to leave the harbor on Monday and the first one to come back on Friday. After the beating the entire crew had taken in the rough waters of the North Atlantic Ocean, none of the guys really cared about the perceptions of people who never, ever braved those frigid, violent swells.

"We're home, boys," Scotty announced right as Mark pulled *Murphy's Law* into the port.

He hopped over the edge, and Matt's heart sunk in his chest. Normal people could've never cleared the distance Scotty had in a single bound, at least not that he'd ever seen.

Chuck yelled out. "Drop the anchor, Skipper."

The dropping of the anchor meant they'd made it home safe and sound.

Home. Well, as close as Matt could be to "home" at the moment. He stepped over the edge of the boat onto the pier, and even though he wasn't exactly on solid ground, it was close enough for comfort, and that was all Matt really needed.

He looked up toward the gray sky, toward heaven, as his mom had always taught him, and thanked whatever power might be up there listening for getting him back ashore safely. There'd been a few times when he'd thought he was destined to die out on those rough open waters, but there he stood—alive and breathing.

The bag strapped to his back slid down his arms, and he immediately knelt down and began digging. He'd promised his mother and promised Luke a phone call when he finally made it back, and he wouldn't miss sharing one second of his safe return with two of the people who meant the most to him.

Holding down the button to turn his phone back on, he watched as a tiny brunette charged up the pier and all but collided with Scotty's massive body. He hugged the woman hard, lifting her up from her feet. She had about half his height and less than a quarter of his size, but Matt could tell by the looks on their faces and their shared joy that they were a perfect fit for each other.

Chuck headed toward Emma's bar. No one was there to greet him, not like Scotty had been met. Emma stopped long enough to give him a hug and welcome him back, but Matt could tell her sights were set on his older brother. She let Chuck go, then took off in a dead run—blonde curls flowing behind her, arms spread wide, an excited smile curling her bright red lips. Matt saw the love and relief in her eyes as her stare landed on his brother, and Mark returned that look tenfold. Despite what Mark claimed, those two were obviously head over heels for each other.

The sight of Scotty and Mark, and the women hugging them so tightly, made Matt wish he had one of his own loved ones there to greet him, to be so overwhelmed with joy he'd made it back safely that they flung themselves at him and held on to him as if he were the last solid being on earth. It made him even more homesick than he'd been before.

The sound of his phone chiming pulled his attention away from all the happy, hugging lovers, and when he looked down at the screen, he found five missed calls from his mother, a text from Luke, a text from Brandon, and three voice mails. It brought the reality of his life crashing down around him with great fury.

"Get the easy stuff out of the way first," he muttered as he swiped his finger over the phone and pulled up the text from Luke.

The message was a simple, "Wanted you to know I was thinking about you. Please be safe out there. Can't wait to see you again."

Matt concurred. He was more than excited to hit the road so he could get back home to the man he'd spent the last twenty or so years of his life being in love with. He couldn't wait to feel Luke's lips against his again, couldn't wait to have Luke in his arms.

The message from Brandon read, "Picked up the car like you asked. Thanks for letting me keep it. You're one of the good ones."

Matt rolled his eyes and deleted the string of messages between him and his former partner. If he wanted to really give things with Luke an honest try, he knew he needed to make sure he was completely over Brandon.

He then pressed his thumb down over the little voice mail icon, and all three voice mails were from his mother. She knew he'd been on a boat, that he wouldn't have cell service out in the middle of the ocean, and even if he did manage to get a weak signal, he wouldn't have time to talk to her. So why the hell leave three messages?

Unless something was wrong....

The oldest unheard message came in on Wednesday. He heard his mom say, "Matty, I know you probably can't get this message, but I thought I should call anyway. There's been an accident. Luke has been rushed to the hospital. I don't know what's happening yet, but I'll call as soon as I do." And that's where the message ended.

Matt's heart stopped beating. He grabbed the post beside him because he didn't trust his legs to hold his weight. *You're overreacting already. It could be nothing. Stay calm*, he silently reminded himself over and over as his phone retrieved the next message.

"It's Mom again. I'm at the hospital with Luke's mom and dad. He was responding to a 911 call, and he was on the fourth floor of the building. The roof caved in on top of him and took the third and fourth floor out. He was stuck in debris. They have him on oxygen right now, and he's not awake, but they're hopeful. Call me as soon as you can."

The last message came in a few short hours before Matt made it back to Portsmouth. It queued up, and he was almost too afraid to listen. That message had a fifty-fifty chance of breaking his heart or leaving him with the possibility of seeing his best friend alive. Again, it was his mother. He heard the sound of her sniffling, and all hope faded away.

"Matty, Luke's in a coma. They say there's swelling on his brain, and according to the MRI, he had a spinal trauma. They don't know the extent of the damage yet, but they say they'll need to do surgery soon. I'm so sorry, sweetie. Call me as soon as you can."

That did it. Matt's legs buckled, and he hit the rough boards of the pier with both knees. If he'd been half-aware of his body, the shock of such a fall might've sent pain rippling through him, but right now, the only pain he felt was in his chest. He doubled over, palms slapping against the wood, and he started to throw up right there in the middle of the pier.

"Matt!" Mark called out from behind him.

Heavy footfalls charged toward him. They were distant, at the end of a long tunnel distant, but coming close fast. Matt's stomach turned. His throat spasmed. He was going to hurl. He just knew it. But before lunch decided to make a return visit, two different sets of strong arms wrapped around him and hefted him up from where he'd collapsed.

"Matt, what's wrong?" his brother asked.

"He looks pale," he heard Scotty say.

"Maybe he needs a hospital," Chuck followed.

"Maybe you guys need to give him some space," Emma countered.

CHAPTER TWENTY-TWO

"LUKE," MATT said in a gravelly voice. "He's been hurt. I need to get home."

"Who the hell is Luke?" Scotty asked.

No one said a word.

"It's his best friend," Mark offered on his brother's behalf. "They've known each other since high school." Mark stopped and set Matt down on one of the back chairs in Emma's restaurant. "Matty, what happened?"

Matt repeated the details of their mother's messages back to Mark. Mark listened carefully, even as Scotty and Emma went searching for something to drink and a cool, damp cloth for Matt's face. The moment the rag touched his skin, it felt like he returned to life. He actually felt like he could breathe again.

"I gotta get home," he said in a pleading voice to the people hovering over him and watching him so intently. "I have to...."

"Calm down," Mark said. "I'll get Emma to book the first flight back to Tennessee, okay?"

Matt couldn't do much more than nod.

They left him sitting alone at the table in the back corner of the restaurant, alone to think about the worst possible thing that could happen and kick himself in the ass for not staying there after Luke had kissed him. At least if he'd stayed, he could be there to hold Luke's hand right now.

Wait.

No, he couldn't. Luke's family had no clue about their son's sexual preference, and the way Matt reacted was more of a terrified lover than a concerned best friend. If he even once mentioned to Luke how much he loved him, even in desperation, and they heard, Luke would be shoved right out of the closet and into the limelight. He couldn't do that to Luke.

Someone had picked up his phone for him, not that he remembered dropping it or the fact he didn't have it glued to the palm of his hand. The display had a crack in it. Not so bad it rendered the phone inoperable, but bad enough it annoyed the little OCD Matt had. He swiped his finger over the screen and pulled up his mother's number, impatiently listened to the sound of the ringing before he heard her voice. "Oh, Matty." She was sniffling again.

"Any news?" he said hoarsely.

"Not yet. They're still running all these tests. I'm sitting with Mrs. Bishop now."

"Mark and Emma are trying to get me a flight home."

"That's great, son. So great."

"If I have Mark call you with the details, can you pick me up from the airport and take me to the hospital?"

"Of course I can."

"Thanks, Mom."

He hung up the phone before his mother had a chance to say anything else. It wasn't that he wanted to cut her off. He didn't do it on purpose. If he had to put blame for his rudeness anywhere, it would be on the zombie he'd turned into since hearing about Luke's accident. His stomach remained knotted, as did the muscles in his neck and shoulders, while he sat there helplessly waiting on someone to give him some news—whether it be of Luke's miraculous recovery or someone finding him a quick flight back to Tennessee.

"There's a flight leaving Portsmouth International in an hour and a half," Emma announced, charging toward the table where Matt had been sitting alone all this time. "Your brother is gassing up the truck, and he's going to take you to the airport. We had to get a first-class ticket, but you'll be home in no time."

Matt stood from his chair, legs still shaky, and he threw his arms around Emma's neck. He held on to her for a long while without saying anything, fearing the moment he actually managed to speak, he might break into tears again. And who wanted to see a grown man crying like a baby?

"It's okay," she whispered, gently dragging her hand up and down his back. "If something happened to Mark, I would be in the same shape."

Her words made Matt raise his head. Why in the hell would she compare what he was going through with Luke to the way she felt about Mark... unless Mark had already told her about his big gay little brother.

"Do you—"

"Know?"

Matt nodded.

"Yeah, I know. He told me about you long before you were supposed to come up here. He talks about you all the time, how proud he is and how much he missed you. I asked him once why you two never saw each other. He then told me about how Constance treated you."

Matt's mouth formed a big, silent O shape.

"I don't have a problem with who you love, sweetheart, as long as you find love. I think everyone deserves to be in love at least once in their life. Don't you?"

"Yeah," Matt said distantly. He'd found his love once, or maybe Luke made it twice. Brandon was obviously the wrong one for him, but that didn't change the fact Matt had loved him wholeheartedly. It just made him foolish enough to believe their love would last forever.

"Hey, you," Emma said as she gently gripped his chin and lifted his head. "He'll be okay. Have a little faith."

"I'm trying. I just need to see him. I need to be there in case... in case...."

"Stop thinking like that, Matthew Jacob Murphy."

Holy shit. Matt hadn't heard his full name said like that since he was a kid, when his mom caught him doing something he wasn't supposed to. Come to think of it, Emma sounded *exactly* like his mother when she said it. Ironically enough, the scolding use of his full name gave him a hint of comfort, as if everything would be okay because he had family—real family—to make sure he was taken care of.

"Woman, what are you doing to my baby brother?" Mark asked.

"She's being a saint," Matt said before Emma had a chance to answer.

"Of course she is. Why else would I fall in love with her?" Mark wrapped his arm around Emma's shoulders and pulled her in for a hug. He kissed her temple, then looked at Matt and said, "I'm ready to go if you are."

"I've been ready."

Mark let his woman go and started toward the door, only Matt wasn't following him. Not yet. He needed to do something before he left, and honestly, he didn't know if he would ever make it back to New Hampshire.

He pulled Emma into a tight hug and held on to her for a moment before finally saying, "Thank you for everything. You've been really good to me."

"You're practically family now, sweetie."

"I'm glad my brother met you. He needed a good one in his life." And that was the absolute truth. It didn't matter that Matt barely knew Emma. He could tell she was one of the good ones, not like Mark's ex, Constance. "Too bad Mark didn't meet you sooner."

"True. Then we wouldn't have to fight to get his kids back."

"Yeah." Matt loosened his hold of her. "I would love to see my niece and nephew again."

"Wouldn't we all? Now, go, and you have a safe trip home, okay?"

"I will."

CHAPTER TWENTY-THREE

THANKFULLY, IT didn't take long for Mark to get Matt to the airport. Even the plane left on time, as if someone with the power to align the universe just right had decided to bat for Matt's team. His nerves were already so fried, the turbulence at takeoff didn't bother him, nor did the jostling down the runway when the plane finally landed at Memphis International.

Matt ran the entire length of the airport, then jogged down the escalator to get to his baggage. He impatiently waited for the one duffel bag he had—an inch and a half shorter and he could've carried the damn thing onboard—watching as the carousel made circle after circle. He was almost to the point of saying screw the bag. He could get more clothes from home, but just before he threw his hands in the air and walked away, his duffel bag appeared. He snatched it from the luggage carousel, then took off through the automatic glass doors leading out into the passenger pickup.

Immediately, he spotted his mom's white Cadillac and a head full of salt-and-pepper hair. She looked to be arguing with a Memphis police officer by the way she waved her arm in the air and the unamused look on his face. "Mom," Matt called from across the parking garage, hurrying toward her. "What are you doing?"

"Well, I *tried* to explain to this fine, upstanding protector and server here that I was waiting for my *son*—" She held her hands out toward Matt but smirked up at the police officer. "—who would be getting off a plane soon, so it was perfectly acceptable for me to park in the *passenger* pickup zone."

"And the problem is…?" Matt asked.

"Your mother has been sitting here too long. I simply asked her to make a circle and come back."

Matt looked down at his mother and arched his brow.

109

"And I told him you have a friend in critical condition at The Med."

"That's the truth," Matt offered. "He's a firefighter, and he fell through two floors of a building after the roof collapsed."

"Oh shit," the cop said—eyes wide, fist curled at his mouth. "I saw that on the news. Come on, I'll get you guys there."

"Oh, sir, there's no need to rush. He's as stable as they can get him right now."

"Maybe, but I ain't got nothin' better to do at the moment."

"Well, what are you waitin' for, sweet cheeks," Matt's mom said. "Hop in that car of yours, turn on them pretty blue lights, and let's go."

Matt hung his head. His mother always did such a great job of embarrassing him, and this situation with the cop was no exception to the general rule.

He climbed into the passenger side of her car and chucked his bag in the floorboard. She climbed into the driver seat beside him. The cop car whipped around to the front of the Caddy, blue lights flashing brightly. Matt laid his head back against the seat and closed his eyes. Everything was just a little too much to deal with right now, even his mom going on and on about the cop who was kind enough to escort them downtown to The Med.

They sped around the I-240 loop from Airways to the Union Avenue exit on the west side of the city. Had they not had the police escort, they would've been deadlocked in Friday afternoon traffic at Malfunction Junction—the place where Interstate 40 and 240 split off, the place where non-Memphians always got turned around and traffic always backed up.

The cop swerved around all the cars moving at a snail's pace and barreled up the ramp. Matt's mom kept the pedal to the metal, the Cadillac keeping the kind of speed it was built for like it was no big deal.

Both cars hauled around the loop leading from the interstate onto Union Avenue, and again, the mass of unsuspecting motorists quickly pulled away. Within a matter of ten minutes, they were pulling up to The Med's emergency entrance. Never in a million years would they have made it that fast during rush hour. Matt had spent close to an hour stuck on that exact route before.

His mother parked the car in one of the pay lots while the cop waited in his car against the curb. Matt climbed out, leaving his bag behind. He approached the squad car as the cop stepped out and stood next to his vehicle. Matt offered him a hand and the officer took it. "Thanks for helping us out," he said. "We would still be back at Airways had you not escorted us."

"Least I could do, man," the officer gave him a firm shake. "If I ever get hurt, I just hope someone'll do the same for my wife and kids."

There it was—understanding. That explained why the cop was so eager to help, even after Matt's mom berated him about the parking situation.

Matt released the cop's hand the moment his mom stepped up to his side, gave the guy a smile, then looked over at his mom. "Can you take me to Luke now, please."

"Absolutely, sweetie. Let's go." She looked at the cop and said, "Thank you for taking the time."

"To protect and serve," the officer said, "that's what I'm here for."

Matt followed his mother as she walked up the sidewalk and into The Med's main entrance. The emergency waiting room overflowed with people waiting for medical attention. The hospital left a whole lot to be desired. The clientele consisted of mostly people with no insurance, who needed to see a doctor for things as small as a common cold. Homeless frequently used the waiting room as shelter from the cold, but The Med had the best trauma ward in the tri-state area. They saved lives, and Matt knew beyond a shadow of a doubt that Luke was in good hands there.

Matt's mother led him over to the hallway leading down to the Elvis Presley Memorial Trauma Center and down to the cleaner, well-guarded waiting rooms where he immediately saw Mr. and Mrs. Bishop sitting in the chairs closest to the coffee pot. Luke's mom had a blanket wrapped around her as she nestled against her husband's side. Luke's father looked completely exhausted as well, but they both smiled and started to stand when they saw Matt.

"No, don't get up for me." He pressed his palms to the air.

"We're glad you could make it," Mr. Bishop said.

"Luke finally woke up," Mrs. Bishop added. "They're taking him into surgery now. He didn't have any feeling in his toes and was complaining about his head hurting."

Closing his eyes, Matt let out a sigh. "Will I be able to see him when they're done with surgery? I really want to be there when he wakes up."

"I'm sure of it," Mrs. Bishop said. "He would love to see your face. He asked if you knew what happened to him. We told him you were flying back in tonight and would be here as soon as you could."

"Thank you."

CHAPTER TWENTY-FOUR

TOO MANY hours passed too slowly. With each little tick of the clock, Matt got more and more antsy. Sitting wasn't an option and pacing didn't help his nerves either. When wringing his hands and sucking down coffee failed, he found himself going back to one of his old bad habits—the very bad habit Brandon despised, the habit Luke always gave him shit over, even though Luke had been the one who'd handed him his first cigarette.

Matt bummed a smoke from one of the nurses he'd found hunkered down on the side of the hospital. She looked like she'd been run through the ringer too. Her eyes were haloed by thick, dark circles. Her shoulders had a definite slump.

"Thanks," he mumbled.

"You look like you need it," she said flatly.

"The same could be said for you."

"One more hour to go," she whispered.

"I wish I could say the same."

She gave him a sorrowful look as she pushed up from the brick wall, then handed him an extra smoke and a spare lighter. "Just in case."

The corner of his lips kicked up in a half smile, the only emotion behind it being gratitude. She nodded, then made a quick exit for the "emergency only" entrance.

Looking down at his hands, he rolled the lit cigarette between his thumb and forefinger, watching ribbons of white smoke billow up from the bright orange cherry at the tip. It took him back to the early days of his friendship with the mysterious new kid in school— Luke, the guy who didn't do the "clique thing," who was so outside of Matt's normal circle of friends, no one knew why Matt had taken to him as quickly as he did. Matt knew. Luke was the most gorgeous guy he'd ever laid eyes on.

He remembered standing behind the gym, hiding from his popular friends with the boy he knew he would fall in love with. Matt had spoken to him probably four times since the guy had first walked into his homeroom in the middle of their tenth grade year. Odd for Matt. He talked to everyone, but there was something much different about the new kid, something that gave him a sincere sense of flutters.

Every time Matt had opened his mouth to speak to Luke, his brain had turned to mush, and his voice couldn't seem to find its life. He turned into a silly boy with a ridiculous crush and feared making a fool of himself. Eventually, though, he pulled himself together enough to approach the boy with a smile as radiant as a California sunrise and hair the color of pure gold. Eventually, he braved the deep blue waters of Luke's curious stare, and thankfully, because of his bravery, they'd eventually become inseparable.

Running his hand up and down his sternum, Matt closed his eyes and silently prayed for Luke. If something happened during surgery and Luke didn't pull through, Matt would never forgive himself for walking away from him after that kiss. He would regret not taking a chance and would never forgive himself for disappointing the best friend and truest love he'd ever had.

He smoked the cigarette down to the butt, then immediately fired up the other one. His hands were shaking so badly every single ash immediately fell away and floated down to the ground.

The sun had already set. Night crept in and consumed the sky. The fall air was cool, cooler than normal for Memphis, but somehow, Matt managed to stay warm. Maybe it was his nerves or the adrenaline pumping through his body. The second cigarette was now long gone, and the only thing Matt had left to do with himself was go back inside. Hurry up and wait… and wait… and wait.

Every hard thump of his boots against the linoleum floors inside the hospital echoed in the wide vacant hallway leading back to the trauma waiting rooms. Matt was in such a weird headspace, he'd nearly stormed right past his mother without even realizing it.

"Honey," she said as she reached for his arm. He lifted his head and all but stared right through her. "You okay?"

Matt shrugged. "As 'okay' as I can be, I guess."

Her lips thinned as she pinched her mouth shut. She had the most sorrowful expression on her face, as though she wanted to take his pain away and hated that she couldn't. "Look," she said as she brushed her hand over his upper arm. "I'm going home. I'll stop by Luke's place and check on Zeus on my way to the condo. Do you need anything? Clothes? Food? Cigarettes?" she said the last with an arched brow. He'd been busted.

"No. I'm fine. I just… want to see Luke right now."

"I know you do, sweetie. You'll see him soon." She pushed up on her tiptoes and just barely managed to reach his cheek. "I love you. Call me if anything changes, 'kay?"

"I love you too. I will."

If he'd thought about it in time, he would've offered to walk his mother to her car, but by the time his brain caught up to his body, she'd already disappeared out the doors. At least the lots had security guards and she'd parked in the one closest to the emergency room entrance. Sighing, he turned back around and continued down the hall and through the double doors of the trauma waiting room.

Most of the people who'd been there when he'd arrived had cleared out. One couple huddled in the corner with a priest or a pastor or one of those guys. It wasn't looking good for whoever they were waiting for. Not that Matt knew the details, but he could tell by the expressions on their faces, they weren't expecting a favorable outcome.

The woman raised her head, and Matt quickly looked away, back over to where Luke's parents were sitting. He couldn't really bring himself to join them either. After all, he'd sort of been lying to them for a long damn time about just how deep his feelings for their son ran, and right now, he felt like he could confess everything without the first ounce of guilt, and that wouldn't be fair to Luke. Not even a little.

The moment he decided to go over to the coffeepot for a third or maybe fifth cup of java, a white-coat-clad doctor stepped into the room and called out, "Mr. and Mrs. Bishop?" Luke's parents both stood from their seats. Matt spun on his heel to face them all. The doc said, "Surgery went well. Luke pulled through just fine," and those were the last words Matt heard.

His heart pounded hard, beating at an almost explosive rhythm in his temples. The trembling in his hands grew stronger, but this time it wasn't from nervousness. He was anxious to see Luke, to stare into his best friend's crystal-blue eyes and hold his hand.

"Is he awake?" Matt blurted, interrupting whatever conversation they'd been in the middle of.

"He's still groggy, but he's awake," the doctor informed.

Matt closed his eyes and took a deep calming breath, let it wind through his lungs and fill his body with relief. He felt a soft, delicate, dainty hand on his forearm, and when he opened his eyes again, he saw Luke's mom staring back at him with a sympathetic look in her eyes.

"You go see him first," she said. "I know he'll be happy you're here."

"Thank you," Matt whispered because he couldn't seem to manage anything more.

The doctor reached for the door and said, "Follow me."

Matt impatiently followed him down the hall, past the trauma patient rooms and the step-down rooms, toward ICU and post-op recovery. He resisted the urge to bolt into a speeding run, resisted breaking away from the ambling doctor and into every single room until he found Luke.

"He's pretty banged up," the doctor warned. "He looks bad, but I promise he's going to be okay. He's in good hands here. The staff is doing the best it can for him."

"I appreciate it, and I know his parents do too."

"We hate to see fallen heroes come through here."

"I can imagine."

The small talk was almost maddening, as maddening as Matt's need to see Luke, but he went along with it. He did the smiling and nodding and the thanking—only because he didn't want to come off as rude.

"You can stay as long as you want," the doctor said as he patted Matt on the back. He twisted the doorknob to Luke's room, then stepped out of the way.

As eager as Matt had been to see Luke, he couldn't step through that door immediately. He had to put his game face on, had to prepare for the worst and hope for the best. He had to ready himself to see the man he didn't want to live without lying on a hospital bed, mangled and broken. Matt had to push back the fear and be the strength Luke would need him to be, no matter how badly he might want to break down and cry.

Matt pressed his palm to the door. The hinges squeaked as he slowly pushed it open. Before he even saw Luke lying in the bed, he heard the *beep beep beep* of the different monitors attached to Luke's frail body. The sound was a grim reminder of how short life could be, too short. And missed chances had the potential to turn into life's biggest regrets.

He exhaled slowly and cautiously stepped into the darkened room. Luke was lying on his stomach with his tan, muscled back exposed. A five-by-five patch of white gauze covered the spot where they'd obviously cut into Luke's back, but he wasn't groaning, didn't appear to be in the slightest pain.

"I hear you," Luke said hoarsely. "And I can kinda see you too."

A little snort of laughter slipped past Matt's lips. Luke sounded completely loopy, voice awkwardly lilting. He had a dopey, glaze-eyed grin on his face.

"You can sit down. I won't bite," Luke added.

"I know. I just… I needed a minute. Ya know?"

"Do I look that bad?"

Honestly, no, Luke didn't look half as bad as Matt had expected him to, but maybe that was the sheer excitement of seeing him alive and hearing his voice more than what Matt actually saw with his own two eyes.

He stepped farther into the room and took a seat next to Luke's bed. Looking closer, he saw the cuts and scrapes and bruises. The entire exposed side of Luke's face had been bruised. Bright red blood pooled in his eye and ate away the white. It was a startling contrast to the icy blue of Luke's iris. His plump, beautiful lips had been lacerated down one side. His cheek was swollen and….

117

Matt had to stop taking stock of Luke's injuries. Each new wound roused new fear and insecurity in him. He almost wanted to demand Luke give up fighting fires, but he knew he didn't have that right.

"It must be that bad," Luke slurred.

"No, I… I was lost in thought. Sorry."

"What were you thinking about?"

Sliding the chair closer to the bed, Matt's mind played through a million different answers to that question—a million not including the truth. "Nothing important," Matt lied. "I'm just glad to see you alive."

Luke held out his arm, obviously struggling to lift it from the mattress. He curled his fingers and lowered his hooded stare to his hand. Matt hesitated. He wanted to do so much more than just hold Luke's hand. It involved a whole hell of a lot of holding on to Luke and never letting go of him again.

CHAPTER TWENTY-FIVE

HOURS LATER, Luke's parents said their good-byes. Luke dozed in and out of consciousness, but Matt didn't leave his side. In fact, Matt never let go of his hand, even as his own limbs and lids became heavy with exhaustion. He wouldn't—no, he couldn't—let Luke go through this mess alone.

The sky just outside of Luke's room had begun to lighten—from the pitch-black of night, to the cobalt color of dawn, to the light blue of early morning. Nurses came and went all throughout the night, taking vitals and giving meds. Luke would wake up enough to grumble incoherently, then pass back out. And Matt stayed through every moment of it.

"You need to sleep," Luke mumbled against his pillow. His fingers tightened around Matt's hand. This time, Luke squeezed a bit harder, as if he were finally getting some of his strength back.

"I'm fine," Matt said, voice gravelly.

"You look like hell."

"Yeah, well, I'm not leaving, so give it up already." Luke laughed softly, but the sound was cut short by him wincing. Matt sat forward in the chair. "You okay?"

"I'm fine. I swear."

Luke's declaration allowed Matt to sit back again, but he wouldn't relax. He couldn't relax. The muscles in his shoulders were knotted, and his back could use some serious adjusting, but he wouldn't complain because his hell was nowhere near as bad as Luke's.

He brushed the calloused tip of his thumb over Luke's scraped knuckles. The skin felt a lot like sandpaper, and Matt wondered if Luke had ever had soft knuckles or if his were well-worn from years of manual labor just like Matt's. He couldn't believe that in all their time together, he'd never held Luke's hand. At least he couldn't remember ever holding Luke's hand.

119

"When they finally let you out of this place," Matt said, "where are you going? Have you decided yet?"

"I don't know. Maybe Mom and Dad's house. From what the doctors are saying, I won't be able to get around on my own for a while."

"Go home with me."

"What?" Luke frowned. Then his eyes grew wide, wider than Matt had seen them since Luke had woken up.

"Go home with me."

"Matt."

"Luke, I'm serious. I want to take care of you."

Luke licked his parched lips, and his lids drooped over his eyes again. His nostrils flared as he drew in a deep breath. "Matt, are you sure you want to be stuck taking care of an invalid? I mean, I don't know when I'll be able to get around on my own again."

"I don't care."

"And there's physical therapy."

"I don't care."

"And there's—"

"What part of 'I don't care' do you not understand?"

"I just want you to be fully aware of what you're getting into, Matt. No surprises. It's… it's gonna suck, and I don't want you hating me when I drive you insane."

"I can't hate you," Matt quietly admitted. He spoke from experience. Hating Luke hadn't happened before Matt had finally managed to find someone to love him. It sure the hell wasn't going to happen now that he'd almost lost him. "I don't want to hate you."

"Let me just go to Mom and Dad's until I get better. When all this is over—"

"No. Don't do that to me."

Matt let go of Luke's hand and stood from the chair. His joints cracked and popped as soon as he took the first step. Shock rippled through his body as he managed the first real movement in way too many hours. With each step he took, he cranked his neck from side to side to pop out the kinks in his spine, but that didn't do a damn thing for his knotted muscles.

Rubbing his hand back and forth across his brow, he arranged and rearranged words, hoping to find some way to convince Luke to let him take care of him during this healing and rehabilitation phase of Luke's recovery. The strategically arranged phrases and promises always fell apart at the big L word.

So stupid.

He'd admitted his feelings more than once, but now, when he really needed to tell Luke how much he loved him, he couldn't do it. He could say things like "I care" and "I'm your best friend" and "I've always loved you," but for some stupid reason he couldn't look at Luke and say "I love you" in that very real, very serious *spend-the-rest-of-their-lives-together* sort of way. The thought of uttering those three little words scared the piss out of him for more than one reason. The most terrifying of all—losing Luke like he'd lost Brandon.

"I need to do this, Luke," he finally admitted. "I need you to want me to do this for you."

"Why?"

Such a simple question. Too bad the answer didn't come as easily. It involved a whole lot of admitting Matt wasn't in the best place right now, that he feared being left alone again almost as much as he feared taking his last breath. He would have to admit to Luke that he planned to use the time it took for Luke to recover to prove that he had it in him to love someone so much he was willing to put his entire life on hold just to nurse that someone back to health. If he could do it, if he could survive the weeks or months or years it took to bring Luke back to 100 percent, then he would know they were strong enough to conquer *anything*... even months and months of being apart because Matt needed to make a living the only way he knew how.

"Matt?" Luke whispered. "Please talk to me."

"I'm trying to figure out how to tell you what's going on inside my noggin." Matt gently rapped his knuckles against the side of his skull. "I have a ton of good reasons, but they all sound horrible."

"Why don't you try being honest?"

"Maybe because I am having a hard damn time being honest with myself."

"Understandable. I guess."

"Will you please just let me do this for you?"

"You packed up everything you own and moved it out of your house, remember? The furniture and everything. Where will we sleep? What will we eat on?"

Of course Matt had forgotten about that. It was part of the past Matt wanted to erase—a past that involved someone who cared so little he would bail on Matt the way Brandon did, a past where Matt hid his feelings from Luke. That wasn't the life Matt wanted to live anymore.

"What about your house?" Matt asked. "Wouldn't you be more comfortable at home?"

"Is that really what you want?"

"Yes. It is."

CHAPTER TWENTY-SIX

IT TOOK a hell of a lot of insisting on Luke's part, but Matt finally left the hospital. He'd spent more than a week there, only leaving long enough to run by his mom's condo in Harbor Town—on the banks of the Mississippi River in downtown Memphis—only staying gone long enough to eat, shower, and change. Then he would turn around and head straight back to The Med.

He stopped by his old house first, just to make sure the place was still standing. When he opened the door, cool stale air wafted out from the opening. The house hadn't been vacant for even a month, yet it felt like it'd been abandoned for years.

Matt peeked through the plastic white miniblinds he'd hung in the windows before leaving to go to New Hampshire, into the backyard where Zeus used to play. The spot of grass where Zeus used to dig up the yard had started to grow back. The trees had shed a good bit of their canopies, leaving a blanket of dried brown leaves to cover the lawn.

"Coming here was a mistake," he said as he let the blinds drop back into place.

The table they'd picked out together was gone from the breakfast nook, along with the couch and loveseat that used to be in the living room. Everything—the pictures and decor, the lamps and rugs—everything that made the place a home was gone. Nothing but empty walls and square footage left behind. It turned his home into nothing more than a house—a building with no heart and soul.

Matt had to get out of there.

Yet he couldn't make himself leave.

He went back to the empty bedroom and lay down on the floor where his bed used to be. That square section of beige carpet was a bit lighter than the rest, not that Matt wouldn't have remembered the place where he'd spent so many nights cuddling with Brandon without it.

With his arms tucked behind his head, he closed his eyes and let his imagination run wild. He could almost hear the shower running and Brandon humming a tune from the bathroom, could almost hear Zeus panting from the corner of the bed while they both waited for "Daddy" to get out of the shower. He could almost smell Brandon's cologne lingering in the air.

Ironically enough, though, it wasn't Brandon he missed as much as the comfort and love and sense of finding where he truly belonged. He craved to have those nights wrapped in someone's arms. He craved the feeling of knowing someone looked forward to seeing him at the end of the day. Could Luke be that guy for him?

Truth be told, the two of them were so much alike, Matt doubted either one of them could survive a relationship together. They would butt heads. They would get in each other's way. Who would cook and clean? Who would fix shit when it broke? Was love enough to make everything else just fall into place?

He thought about the titanium band he'd spent a small fortune on and everything that band stood for. He'd been ready to commit himself to one man, to make a vow, "'til death do us part" and all that shit, to someone who could so easily walk away from him. What did that say for his ability to make sound judgments with his love life? If he walked that road with Luke, would the same thing happen? Would he lose the only true friend he had left?

And what about Aric? The sex was great. Neither one of them had any expectations, or did they? Did Aric expect a phone call and a repeat performance? Would it hurt Aric's feelings if Matt didn't want the same?

With a sigh, he pushed up from the bedroom floor and headed back into the hallway, past the room that was once Brandon's writing space, past what used to be Matt's man cave. He stepped over the threshold and into the living room where the afternoon sun leaked through the blinds. Particles of dust danced in the golden rays of light. If he and Brandon still lived in that house, a speck of dust wouldn't have been found.

The phone in his pocket rang. Matt contemplated ignoring it. He didn't trust his voice not to quiver, not to give his sadness and confusion away. If it wasn't for Luke being released soon—according to the myriad of doctors who visited him daily—Matt would've pressed the little button to decline the call and gone on his merry way. But he just couldn't bring himself to do that.

"Hello?" he said without even checking the caller ID because he was too concerned with keeping himself as stoic as possible.

"They're letting me go," Luke said. "The doctors were happy with my reflexes and the hundred and something tests they ran, so they said I could go. I'm just waiting on paperwork to sign and someone to bring me some crutches to take home, then I can leave."

"Crutches?"

"Yeah, they said I need to use them as much as I can stand to get around. Said it will help my recovery and the strengthening… yada yada yada… or something. Mom caught the details. I think I'm still high."

"I can understand that. I'm at my house. I'll head your way now." Luke didn't say anything immediately, and Matt didn't understand the silence. "You still there?" he asked.

"Yeah, I…." He could hear the deep inhale Luke breathed in. Luke held it, then exhaled slowly. "Matt, I can still go to my parents' house. It's not too—"

"No. No, that's not what I want. Is that what you want?"

"Not at all."

"Then why keep bringing it up?"

"I'm giving you an out. I keep expecting you to take it, but you don't."

"Wouldn't that tell you to stop offering?"

"It should, but I can't help worrying that you're going to get tired of taking care of me, and you'll end up resenting me for this."

Ouch. "I'm not that guy, and you know it."

"True. Well, I'll be here waiting for you."

"I'll be there soon."

"Okay. See you soon."

I love you.

Swallowing down those three little words he couldn't bring himself to utter yet, Matt ended the call, then slipped the phone into his pocket. He fished out the keys to the house he still owned but had easily abandoned. Matt left the house and locked everything up tight before he climbed into the rental car his mom had deposited for him while Matt was at the hospital with Luke.

Matt pulled out of the drive, then out of his neighborhood, heading west down Poplar Avenue. He cut over a few streets, and before he knew it, he was in Cooper-Young—the historic district where Luke lived in the first house his parents had ever bought together.

It was a 1930s craftsman, updated with more energy-friendly windows and doors, central heating and air, and a much better plumbing system than they had back when the house was first built. Matt had been in the house a million times before, but walking in there now felt different. This place was about to become his home… at least temporarily.

He pulled all the way into the driveway. Zeus started barking the moment the dog heard the car door slam. Matt walked over to the wooden privacy fence. He heard Zeus scratching at the boards. "It's okay, buddy. Daddy's home." The dog began to bark louder. Matt could see his shadow moving back and forth between the spaces in the wooden fencing.

He unlocked the gate with the one of the many keys Luke had given him, and the moment the door swung open, Zeus lunged every ounce of his fifty pounds at Matt. The puppy practically jumped into Matt's arms. The force pushed Matt back on his ass, not that he really fought to stay on his feet.

The pit bull pup plied Matt's face with sloppy wet licks, and Matt couldn't do much more than laugh. "It's good to see you too, buddy." He hugged the dog, even as it kicked and wiggled around in his lap. And that's exactly what Matt needed to make him feel like he'd finally made it back home.

"I gotta go, buddy," Matt said as he scratched the dog behind the ears. "Gotta go get Luke from the hospital." Matt stood from the ground, and the puppy whimpered. It followed him all the way over to the gate, and when Matt shut the door, Zeus started to whine. He couldn't stand it. The sound was absolutely heartbreaking. "I'll be back," he said as he climbed into Luke's truck.

CHAPTER TWENTY-SEVEN

WHEN MATT got back to the hospital, he found Luke sitting on the edge of the bed with his legs hanging off the side. The back of his hospital gown flapped open enough for Matt to see the slowly healing scrapes and yellowing bruises. A patch of white gauze still covered the wound from Luke's surgery.

Matt slowly stepped around the bed but didn't say anything. Luke gripped the edge of the mattress so hard his knuckles turned white. He stared down at his bare feet, but somehow, within that stoic expression Matt saw a hell of a lot of desperation.

"What are you doing?" he asked softly.

Luke sighed as he raised his head. He didn't look up at Matt, but rather at the window across the room. "I thought I would try walking, but…."

"By yourself? Have you lost your mind?"

"I can barely feel my feet, Matt."

Those few little words and the sadness in Luke's tone broke Matt's heart. The whole situation had to be driving Luke insane. He'd always been a very independent sort of guy, never really relied on anyone for anything, and now he couldn't even walk across the room without having help. Matt couldn't begin to imagine the frustration.

Matt knelt down on the floor in front of Luke. The cool of the linoleum seeped through his jeans. He took one of Luke's dangling feet into his hand and brushed his thumb over the hard bone of Luke's ankle. Luke didn't even flinch.

"Can you feel that at all?" Matt asked in a hushed voice.

"A little. It feels like a feather."

Was that a good sign? Matt didn't know. At least Luke felt something.

He leaned in closer and pressed his lips to Luke's calf, then moved up to the inside of his knee and up to his exposed thigh. Luke licked his lip, then slowly exhaled. Matt sat straight up on his knees, wrapped his arms around Luke's waist, and buried his face against Luke's stomach. "We'll work through this," Matt vowed. "I'll be there, I promise, and you'll get back to your old self."

He felt Luke's hand brush over the back of his head, and Matt closed his eyes. He tightened his hold on Luke, silently swearing to God nothing would ever make him let go. The big L word trembled on the curve of his lips. He loved Luke, knew and felt it as clearly as he felt his own heartbeat, and yet he still couldn't bring himself to say it out loud.

"Matt," Luke whispered, still brushing his hand over Matt's hair. "I believe you'll do everything you can, but if you get to a point where you can't handle this anymore, promise to tell me, okay? I won't be hurt or mad. Just promise me you won't drive yourself crazy trying to worry over me all the time."

Just as Matt was about to tell Luke he would always worry about him and no amount of promising would stop that, he heard the hinges of the door squeak. Matt raised his head in time to see Luke's parents walk through the door. Mrs. Bishop looked like she'd seen a ghost. Mr. Bishop blanched. And only then did Matt realize how compromising everything looked.

He released his hold of Luke, jumped to his feet and took a step back. His mouth opened and closed. He didn't know what to say or where to begin.

"Is everything okay?" his mother asked a bit breathlessly.

"No. It's not okay," Luke bit back. "I can barely feel my fucking feet."

Matt's throat knotted, and his eyes widened. He couldn't believe the way Luke barked at his mother and couldn't believe he used such a tone and such words to take the focus off the fact they'd just been caught in a more than friendly embrace.

"Matt touched my feet," Luke added. "Touched my calf, knee and thigh, and I didn't feel hardly anything until he touched above my knee. I thought the surgery was supposed to fix that."

"It is, son," his dad said as he stepped forward. "It's going to take some time, though. You can't expect an overnight miracle."

"It's been a damn week, Dad!"

"We know, honey," his mom said as she sat down beside him and took his hand.

Matt felt like he was seriously about to lose his lunch. "I'm going to be outside." He thumbed over his shoulder. Everyone in the room raised their heads and turned their stares to Matt. Luke's parents had a *well-what-are-you-waiting-for* expression on their faces. Luke just looked like he wanted to be saved.

With his pulse pounding hard and his hands shaking, Matt made his escape. Crisis averted. If Luke wanted to explain to his parents what they'd just seen, that was his business. It wasn't Matt's place to yank his best friend out of the closet. God only knew how Luke's parents would react to the news of their son's unholy taste for the same sex.

Fuck! Matt needed a smoke.

No, he needed to man the hell up and stop running away from the hard stuff.

As he pushed through the hospital's glass doors and into the cool November afternoon, he thought about what it would be like to actually be with Luke—in front of Luke's parents, holding hands and occasionally stealing a quick kiss. He'd always felt comfortable being that way in front of his own mother with Brandon and would definitely feel more than comfortable with Luke. But would they ever share their happiness with the people who gave Luke life?

Doubtful.

Matt reached in his leather jacket and grabbed the pack of smokes he'd bought on his first trip away from the hospital almost a week ago. He had four left out of the twenty it came with, proof that all of this mess had been getting to him a lot more than he realized. He put the butt between his lips, then held a lighter's flame to the tip and pulled hard.

The nicotine rush felt pretty damn amazing, so amazing his eyes rolled back in their sockets. Matt wasn't proud of his newfound weakness, but he was quickly becoming a fan of the relief he felt after taking that first drag.

He leaned against the brick wall outside the hospital—the same place where the staff hid to steal their fixes between patients—and he watched each ribbon of smoke ascend toward the sky and become lost in the depressing blue-gray atmosphere surrounding the brick facade. He tried to keep his mind off what could possibly be happening back in Luke's room, but the more he thought about it, the more he worried that Luke would soon find himself with nobody but Matt to take care of him. That wasn't fair. Luke was a hero in the truest sense of the word.

The cell phone in his pocket vibrated, and when Matt checked the screen he saw a message from Luke's phone. It said, "Can you please come back inside?"

Of course he could, but what would he be walking into? He hadn't seen Luke's parents leave. Or did they slip by without him noticing? Would he get his ass chewed the moment he stepped through the door?

Exhaling the last drag he'd taken from the cigarette, he flicked the used butt across the parking lot like everyone else seemed to be doing, then turned and headed back into the hospital. He didn't rush back to Luke's room. In fact, staff raced by him as if he were standing still. He couldn't help his lack of urgency. Somehow, he knew facing what they'd walked in on was going to end up being one giant shit-storm, and he'd probably end up saying something hateful out of spite. Then again, maybe Luke's parents had left, and the fact Matt was knelt down in front of Luke, hugging him for dear life wasn't brought up again. Though, Matt sincerely doubted it.

Before he realized how far he'd gone, he was standing in front of Luke's door again, listening through the thick wood in hopes of getting an idea of what kind of disaster awaited him. He couldn't hear any voices and took that as a good sign. Relief made his hands stop shaking and made his pulse stop racing. But when he stepped into Luke's room, he found Luke's father glaring and his mother sniffling back her tears.

CHAPTER TWENTY-EIGHT

RUN! GO now! Turn back while you still have your balls intact!
Every single instinct in Matt's brain told him to get out now, before
Mr. Bishop had a chance to slug him right in the kisser. But his body
froze where he stood. He couldn't think, and if Mr. Bishop attacked,
Matt knew he wouldn't be able to react in time to get away.

"I told them," Luke said flatly, meeting Matt's bewildered stare
with something resembling silent pleading.

Well, no shit. As if the looks on their faces weren't enough to
give *that* away.

Matt didn't know what to say or do. He wanted to sit down next to
Luke and hold his hand. He wanted to play the strong, supportive role.
But on the other hand, he wanted to run right back out of that room and
pretend none of this had happened. The only thing he could manage
was averting his eyes and keeping his trap shut. If he opened his mouth
now, the wrong thing would come out, and a riot would ensue.

The silence in the suddenly cramped room became absolutely
smothering. Mr. and Mrs. Bishop's distance—their cold glares and
pursed lips, their tense bodies and tightened jaws—made Matt wish
he'd never knelt down on that floor and never kissed along Luke's
leg. If he'd just waited until he had Luke home, none of this would've
ever happened.

"Will one of you please say something?" Luke asked, frustration
and annoyance filling his voice. "We're going to have to talk about
this someday. Why not now?"

"I'd rather do this when you're well," his mother whispered.

"Why? So it'll be easier for you to hate me?"

"Luke!" his father growled.

"What? It's the truth. I saw how the two of you reacted when
you caught us. I watched the way Mom paled and you clenched your

jaw when I said I was in love with Matt. Tell me you weren't sickened. Tell me you didn't want to curse me for this."

The bickering between Luke and his parents became background noise the moment Matt heard Luke say he was in love with him. He couldn't recall Luke ever admitting that before. Sure, they'd owned up to having shared feelings, but being in love? That was a new development. Not one Matt would ever complain about, but new all the same.

Absently, Matt took a step back. He found himself leaning against the wall, biting his tongue real damn hard. As far as he was concerned, he didn't have a say in this argument. Oh, he would put up a fight if it came to it, but Luke needed to hash this out without Matt inserting his two cents.

"Matt?" Luke called out from the bed.

"Huh?" Matt shook his head in an effort to join the here and now.

"You okay?"

"Yeah, I...." He looked away from Luke, over to Luke's parents who were still staring at him like he'd grown a third eye in his forehead. They hated him for this, probably blamed him for "turning" their son into some kind of homo.

God, the thought just pissed Matt off. Their son was a fucking hero. Didn't he deserve to be treated like one? The time had come for him to man up and show Luke just how far he was willing to go to be supportive.

He pushed up from the wall and went right back to Luke's bed. Carefully, he sat down and laid his hand on his knee—palm up, fingers slightly curled. He gave Luke a pleading look, one that begged for him to take his hand. Luke did. Matt inhaled sharply, then turned his stare back to Luke's parents.

"The truth is," he began. "I've loved Luke from the moment I met him. I spent the better part of twenty years loving him, and even when I tried to stop, I couldn't. He has always had a piece of my heart and always will, and if he's willing to give me a chance, then I will do my damnedest to make sure he feels that love for the rest of his life."

The corners of Luke's lips lifted in a small smile. Their fingers tightened, more by Luke's doing rather than his own. His chest suddenly felt constricted, and his pulse raced a little faster. His mouth dried, and he began nervously tapping his foot against the linoleum floor. The rhythm matched the speed of his pounding heart as he turned his gaze over to Luke.

He needed to do it. He needed to finally say the three little words he'd been holding back. Despite what he kept telling himself, he was ready to be in love again, in love with the one person who had always been his everything. The man sitting beside him wouldn't abandon him for no damn reason, wouldn't break his heart with a Dear John letter, and wouldn't leave him to pick up the pieces of their broken home.

One last exhale, Matt looked Luke in the eyes and said an airy, "I love you."

CHAPTER TWENTY-NINE

EVERYTHING HAPPENED so slowly, like staring down a crystalline tunnel and climbing toward a light that just couldn't be reached. One second Matt and Luke were staring at each other blissfully content in the idea of being in love. The next, Matt was tumbling off the bed and hitting the solid floor hard enough to see stars when he opened his eyes again.

Mrs. Bishop screamed.

Luke yelled.

Mr. Bishop punched Matt in the jaw again.

At the moment of impact, Matt tasted bitter, metallic blood on his tongue. The back of his skull cracked the floor. Mr. Bishop fell on top of him, straddling him and angrily spitting his words. "You sick son of bitch! How could you? Luke was perfectly normal until he met you."

All Matt could do was hold up his arms and protect his face.

He heard someone yell for security but couldn't make out the voice for all the crying and screaming in the background. If someone didn't stop Mr. Bishop, Matt would, and it would end up being ugly and violent, and thank God they were in a hospital, because one of them would need it. He didn't want to hit Luke's father, didn't want to start a war between them, but he damn sure wouldn't lie there and get his ass pulverized either.

Matt bucked one good time and dumped Mr. Bishop onto the floor. Somehow, despite the dizziness, he bounded to his feet and held up his fists, ready to strike if Luke's dad so much as tried to get up again.

A set of strong arms wrapped around Matt's torso and yanked him backward. Two more huge, muscled men in black grabbed Mr. Bishop and pulled him toward the far corner of the room. Matt seethed. Mr. Bishop glared. Mrs. Bishop sobbed.

"Get him out of here," Luke said, stabbing his finger in his father's direction. "He attacked Matt, and I want him gone."

"Luke!" his father and mother said in unison, as if they were shocked he would pick Matt's side over theirs.

"I don't want to hear it. Matt didn't deserve that, and frankly, until you both can accept me for me, I don't want to see either of you."

"Come on," Mr. Bishop ordered as he grabbed his wife's hand. "He wants us gone, we'll be gone."

Luke's mother followed, though Matt could tell by the look on her face that she didn't want to go. She didn't want to leave her only son in that hospital and didn't want him to be angry with her. There was an unmistakable sorrow in her glistening blue eyes. Tears clung to her thick brown lashes. But she didn't stop that violent, angry man from dragging her out of the room and essentially, out of Luke's life.

"I'm so sorry," Luke said as he tightened his fists on the edge of the mattress. "I never thought my dad would attack anyone. Had I known, I wouldn't have said shit to him."

The guards loosened their death grip on Matt. One stayed inside the room while the other stepped into the hall. Like they were making sure all was actually well before vacating the scene. Smart. Matt didn't trust Mr. Bishop not to come back for round two.

"I think we're good," the guard in the hallway called back into the room. "But I'm gonna head down just to make sure."

The second guard mumbled toward his colleague, then turned back and gave Matt a nod, not a *sorry for all this shit* or whatever, but acknowledgment that the crazy was over. Good thing too. Luke didn't need any of this crap.

As soon as they were alone again, Matt stepped closer to the bed, close enough so Luke could reach out and hold his hands. Their fingers intertwined again, and Matt felt like he could finally resume normal breathing. The hardest part of Luke's coming out ended with a bloodied lip, but at least Mr. Bishop hadn't hurt Luke. Matt might've genuinely tried to kill him for that.

"It's okay," he said, thumbing the blood from his busted lip. "He needed to know, I guess. At least now you don't have to hide."

"Not from them, I don't. Not that they'll ever talk to me again."

"Your mom will come around. Don't worry."

"How do you know?"

"I could tell by her expression. She didn't want that to happen. Just give them both some time."

"Time. Yeah," Luke said flatly as he laid his head against Matt's stomach.

Admittedly, Luke's openness now, the way he cuddled against Matt and held his hand, surprised the hell out of Matt. Luke had never been the kind of guy—at least not that Matt knew—to get into any kind of PDA. Not that Matt would complain about it. He liked feeling Luke hugged against him. He liked knowing Luke wanted him near.

Screw that. He *loved* it.

"Let me see what the holdup is. I know you're ready to get home."

"Thanks," Luke said as he released Matt's hands and sat back on the bed.

Out in the hallway, a few doctors and nurses stood around the nurses' station. They all looked busy—filling out charts and talking to each other about patients. He almost hated interrupting them, but he had to get Luke out of that damn place and into his own bed. Matt clamped his hands together and leaned his arms against the counter, only slightly annoyed with the idea of waiting for someone to acknowledge him.

One tiny pale-haired nurse with rosy cheeks and a wide, genuine smile raised her head. "Can I help you?" she asked, voice singsong and filled with the same bubbly sweetness as her expression.

"Yeah, my friend, Luke Bishop, is supposed to be released today—"

"The firefighter?"

"Yes, ma'am," Matt answered politely, tone calm and cool. "Anyway, we're wondering what the holdup is. He's really ready to get out of here. The guy's itchin' to be in his own bed again."

"I can imagine." She looked down and thumbed through the stacks of files on the corner of the desk. "Ah, okay. Here it is," she said as she pulled one file out of the middle of the stack. She cracked it open, and her light green stare bounced up and down the page. "Looks like we're just waiting for a wheelchair. If you want, you can go ahead and pull up to the double doors. We'll get him ready for you."

"Thank you," Matt said before returning to Luke's room.

Luke didn't look any better. In fact, the expression on his face seemed a bit sadder. Christ, if only Matt could take that pain away.

Matt's own coming out hadn't been quite as bad, but damn sure hadn't been a walk in the park. Old Man Murphy insisted his son wouldn't be "no damn fairy." Mark pretty much kept his mouth shut while their father yelled homophobic slurs across the room, as did their mother. But when his father finally got the yelling and cursing out of his system, he'd pulled Matt into a hug and told him, "I still love you, son. I may not agree with your lifestyle, but I still love you."

It took quite a few years for their father to truly accept the fact that Matt's sexual orientation wasn't a choice, nor was it some hedonistic lifestyle Matt had chosen just to defy his parents' good Catholic upbringing, but eventually he did. In fact, the first time Matt brought a serious boyfriend home—Brandon—his father welcomed him with a tight hug and a smooch on the cheek. Matt guessed his father learned that some things just weren't important when your time on earth was drawing to a close.

"I didn't hear you come in," Luke said, glancing over his shoulder at Matt. "You okay?"

"Yeah, just remembering Pops is all."

"Sorry," Luke quietly offered.

"No. Don't be. He was miserable in those last months, remember? He didn't want to live like that. You know he couldn't stand having people take care of him."

Luke snorted. "I sympathize."

"Don't be like that. You'll get back on your feet in no time. I'll make sure of it." Matt brushed his hand over Luke's bed-tousled short blond hair, then leaned down and pressed a chaste kiss to his forehead. "They're sending a wheelchair now. I'm going to take as much as I can down to the truck and pull around to the doors. You okay to stay here alone?"

"Yeah. Go. The sooner they get here, the sooner I'll be home."

CHAPTER THIRTY

ALL THE flowers and balloons and "Get Well Soon" pomp had been unloaded from the truck and strategically placed around Luke's not-so-huge midtown home. The fire department sent a massive bouquet of red and white roses, a bunch of balloons, and a huge card that everyone at their station signed. Their wives all got together and bought him an equally impressive floral arrangement and giant box of chocolates that Luke had yet to touch. Matt wanted to set everything up where Luke could see it—like back in the bedroom—but there just wasn't enough room. Besides, if Matt had his way, Luke wouldn't be spending every hour of every day locked away in that room.

Matt had successfully tucked Luke into bed with little aggravation. Luke cooperated well. He never complained and never put up a fight. "I think I'm gonna hit the couch and take a nap," he said as he pulled the last thick blanket up to Luke's chin. "I'll get the heat going too. It's too cold in here."

"You don't have to sleep on the couch. There's plenty of room on the bed."

"Yeah, but you need your rest, and I was going to let Zeus in."

Luke laughed. "Zeus usually sleeps in the bed with me."

"Oh." Matt chuckled softly. "If you don't think we'll make you uncomfortable…."

"Not at all. In fact, I sort of miss him."

"Then I'll be right back."

He kissed Luke's forehead one last time, then left the darkened bedroom and headed back through the house, past all the reminders of Luke's accident, past the kitchen table where they'd shared more than a few beers and a few weighty conversations in the past. Matt looked down at the dark, black wooden surface, and for some reason, a particular conversation he'd had with Luke a few years ago came to mind.

Brandon had gotten really mad at him about staying out late after being gone for a few weeks. Matt had tried to explain that he needed to see his friends too, had even invited Brandon to come along, but Brandon had declined. He'd sat at the table with Luke, guzzling down his fifth or sixth beer in less than an hour and had a pretty decent buzz going. Why he'd never noticed the way Luke looked at him then was beyond him now. Maybe he'd been too drunk to catch on. But he remembered Luke saying something to the effect of, "There's someone better for you, and one day, you'll open your eyes and see him."

That night, Matt had dismissed what Luke had said, but now it made so much sense. Years had passed, and the subject never came up again. Their weighty conversations had less to do with their love lives and more to do with the passing of Matt's father or stupid accidents Luke got himself into, and even the topic of Mark's homophobic wife and how Matt missed his brother came up from time to time. Looking back on those conversations, it seemed like every time Brandon came up, Luke changed the subject. Now Matt understood why.

"So stupid," he muttered as he moved on from the table and toward the door leading into the backyard.

Zeus sat back on his haunches, staring up at a tree as if he were watching and waiting for someone or something to come down and play with him. The moment the dog heard the door open, his head whipped back, and he launched into a gallop. He charged right for Matt, and the force pushed Matt back inside the house.

Matt laughed as he knelt down and pulled Zeus into a hug. The pup's paws pressed against each pec. Zeus greedily licked Matt's jaw and neck and cheeks and nose. He was happy to see his daddy again, and God, did his daddy miss him too.

"C'mon, buddy," Matt said as he climbed back to standing. The pit bull hopped and bounced in circles at his feet, panting and whimpering, begging daddy to play with him. Zeus kept up the playful routine all the way back to Luke's bedroom. Matt opened the door, and the puppy immediately made a beeline for the bed.

"Zeus!" Matt called out when he saw the dog pounce on Luke's chest and saw Luke's hard wince. The puppy paid him no attention, though. "Get down!"

"It's okay. He's fine," Luke hoarsely offered. "This is a normal night for us."

"Before you were hurt."

"I don't want to be treated like glass, Matt."

"And I understand that, but you still have stitches in your back, and you're not—"

"Matt...."

"Not glass," Matt said with a sigh. "Got it."

Matt kicked out of his boots as he shed his leather jacket. He bent down and grabbed the steel-toed shoes and moved them out of the middle of the floor, just in case Luke got a wild hair for adventuring. The last thing they needed was for Matt's lack of precision neatness to cause any more accidents. He laid his jacket over the arm of a corner chair, then pulled his shirt over his head and tossed it on top of the growing pile. Matt glanced over only once to make sure Luke was okay, and that's when he found his best-friend-turned-love-interest staring at him.

"Sorry, I thought... I could change in another room."

"Why? Am I making you uncomfortable?"

"God, no. I thought I was making you uncomfortable."

"No." Luke shook his head. Matt caught the shadow of his smile in the dim light of the table lamp beside him. The sight had an almost warming effect on Matt's heart.

"Do you want me to sleep beside you tonight?"

"Please."

"I sleep naked."

"Normally, I do too."

"You should've told me. I would've taken care of those clothes for you."

"I'm telling you now."

CHAPTER THIRTY-ONE

COMPLETELY NAKED, Matt stalked over to the bed where Luke lay twisted in the sheets. Though Luke didn't have enough strength to walk, he still had the ability to move his arms and legs. The thought of stripping Luke out of his clothes excited Matt in a way he hadn't expected. After all, this was supposed to be about caring for his injured best friend, not satisfying some salacious craving he'd had for the last twenty or so years. He had to keep silently reminding himself of Luke's stitches and his bruises and scrapes and....

Yes, that did it. Thinking of putting Luke through any more pain tamped down Matt's raging libido and put the kibosh on any lewd thoughts... at least for the moment.

He peeled back the covers, then climbed onto the bed and knelt beside Luke while the puppy curled at the foot. Luke stared up at Matt, seemingly watching his every move, as if Luke didn't want to miss a moment of this interaction.

Slowly, gently, Matt eased his hands beneath the hem of Luke's T-shirt. He felt the firm rippled mounds of Luke's abs against his palm, but he also felt the rough slivers of scar from all the injuries Luke had sustained over the years. He pushed away those thoughts as he pushed Luke's shirt up over his body.

"Why didn't we do this sooner?" Matt asked, though it wasn't a question that warranted an answer, more internal monologue spilling out from his lips.

"Because I was an idiot," Luke said.

"I think we were both a little idiotic in this case."

Matt lifted the shirt over Luke's head and brought his hands back down to free him of his sleep pants. Luke caught him by one wrist, pulled Matt's balled fist up to his mouth, and pressed a lingering kiss to Matt's knuckles—lips caressing his flesh. When he looked up, his cool blue gaze met Matt's, and Matt's breath caught in his throat. The culmination of twenty years of friendship, love, and fighting not to love, came down to this one moment.

Matt found himself completely at a loss for words. Oh, there was plenty to say. Plenty of declarations and vows could've been made. He might've even gone as far as to whisper sweet nothings into Luke's ear, but he'd completely lost his voice. His mouth opened and closed, that he was aware of, but he couldn't bring himself to shatter such a sweet moment with the noise of words. Luke did that for him.

"It broke my heart when you became serious with Brandon, ya know?"

Matt lowered his head and closed his eyes. His voice came out in a soft, almost shattered sort of sound. "I didn't know about… about you. I mean…."

"I know. I'm sorry for that. I wish I could've been strong enough to admit how I felt sooner. It scared me, though. I mean, I knew Dad would react the way he did. I was just putting off the inevitable."

"It's done now. Stop worrying and relax. Let me take care of you, and we'll figure everything else out as we go."

Luke nodded, and Matt went back to removing his sleep pants. He hooked his fingers around the waistband and slowly slid them down over Luke's hips and down his thighs. Only a thin pair of briefs covered that massively impressive bulge between Luke's thighs.

"Take those off too, please," Luke asked.

Matt looked up and was met with the darkest, most lust-filled stare he'd ever seen from Luke. It conjured all sorts of sordid fantasies— fantasies Matt had tried to forget. The look and the long-forgotten fantasies roused Matt's desire. He had to look away to compose himself.

"You okay?" Luke asked.

"Perfectly fine," Matt croaked. He smiled, though his lips felt tense and tight, and he reached out for Luke… to undress Luke.

As he pulled the briefs down, the length of Luke's flaccid cock slowly became exposed. Matt thought of a hundred different things he could do to help Luke get hard, ways he could fondle, touch, kiss, and caress the man he loved, if that's what Luke wanted from him.

Damn if Matt wouldn't mind doing any one of those cleverly carnal things to Luke's body.

He tossed the briefs off to the side of the bed to join the rest of Luke's clothes, and for a moment, he fought not to look back at Luke. The moment he did, he knew he would want to make love to Luke, or even have Luke make love to him, and they couldn't have that. Not with Luke "taking it easy" so he could fully recover from his two-story fall.

Then Luke said, "Why won't you look at me?"

"Because I want you bad enough already."

"Then it has nothing to do with me being hurt?"

"It has everything to do with you being hurt." Matt finally raised his head. He found Luke's face turned away, as if he were staring out the window at the other end of the room because he couldn't bring himself to look at Matt. "I don't want to do anything to mess up whatever the doctors did to you."

"I told you"—Luke finally looked back at him—"I'm not made of glass."

No, he wasn't. The proof was in all the monumental accidents Luke had survived, the catastrophes he'd walked away from with no more than a few cuts and bruises. The proof was in the fact Luke was still alive.

Matt wrapped his fingers around Luke's softened shaft and slowly began to stroke. "I've always wanted to touch you like this," he whispered before pressing his lips to the firm muscle just beneath Luke's right pec. "I've always wanted to have you completely naked in the bed with me." He waved his fingers over Luke's hardening erection as he trailed kisses down his lover's abs.

"Please, don't stop," Luke said in a winded voice. "Please. I've wanted this for a long time too, Matt. Don't stop now."

It was too late to stop now anyway. Matt staked his claim and had already begun moving in. He kissed the patch of dirty-blond hairs sprinkled around Luke's navel, then kept going lower and lower, lower until his lips brushed over the top of Luke's thick shaft. He licked down to the tip of Luke's cock, wound his tongue around the head, then took every single firm inch into his mouth.

143

As soon as he heard Luke moan, he felt a hand knot in his hair. The grip wasn't tight, not as tight as someone of Luke's strength should've been able to grip, and despite the cock buried deep in Matt's mouth, Luke's weakened hold concerned him.

Just don't think about it right now, Matt silently encouraged himself. *Just give Luke what he wants, and tomorrow you can work on his other needs.*

Matt bobbed his head up and down as he swirled his tongue around Luke's thickness. His own cock began to ache with need. God help him, he wanted to be inside Luke, making love to him, stroking him, bringing him to orgasmic bliss. He'd never wanted anyone as badly as he wanted Luke Bishop, and now, with his mouth around Luke's shaft and his hand on his own erection, he craved Luke more than he ever had before.

"Yes. Yes. Yes," Luke rasped, opening his legs so Matt could really get close.

He took Luke to the hilt, licking and sucking. He felt the warmth of precum on his tongue and drew those slick droplets down Luke's erection. He lapped, toyed and tickled, tracing the veins rolling down Luke's cock with the firm tip of his tongue as he massaged his lover's sac with a few strong fingers.

"I'm about to come!" Luke cried, and Matt didn't stop.

He bobbed his head faster, stroked his own cock harder. The moment that bitter heat hit his tongue, Matt swallowed it down. Every single drop. Not one bit wasted. Before too long, his own release spilled into his hand, and he joined his lover in postcoital bliss.

CHAPTER THIRTY-TWO

THE DAY before Thanksgiving—close to two weeks since Luke had come home from the hospital—Luke still hadn't spoken to his parents. They planned to spend the holiday with Matt's mom instead. She'd said she would come over and cook dinner for the boys, and as a special treat, Mark and Emma planned to come to town too. Mark had told Matt a few days ago that it was high time their mom met the woman Mark was falling in love with.

Luke's physical therapy moved along nicely. He could now walk around with the help of crutches, but he tired quickly. Luke was stubborn as ever, though. Even though his body wanted to give up, he kept pushing.

The phone on the end table rang. Matt didn't want to answer it. They were well into a movie that had just gotten good, and they both had their eyes glued to the screen. It was the first down day they'd had in far too long, and Matt really only wanted to forget about everyone and everything other than Luke.

It rang again, and Matt groaned.

"I can pause it," Luke offered.

"Please," Matt said as he leaned over to check the caller ID. It was Luke's parents, and Matt sure the hell didn't want them ruining the evening they'd been having. It was a good night—a pain-free night, a fun and quiet night.

"Who is it?" Luke asked.

"Relax. I got it. I need to let Zeus in anyway."

Matt grabbed the phone and headed into the kitchen before he dared answer it. He stepped out into the backyard, and he answered the phone with a curt, "Hello?"

"Why in the hell are you answering Luke's phone?" Mr. Bishop all but growled.

"Because I've been taking care of your son," Matt said flatly.

"You mean the man you turned into a homo?"

"I mean the hero who almost lost his life trying to save people from a burning building."

Silence. Not that he expected Luke's father to say anything to that. He couldn't argue the fact his son was a genuine hero. The Memphis fire department had even presented Luke with an award and everything. It was official and undeniable, and not even the good word of Mr. Holier-Than-Thou could take that away from Luke.

"Any particular reason you called?" Matt finally asked.

"As a matter of fact," Mr. Bishop responded, "I want the two of you out of my house. You have thirty days."

"You're kidding!" Matt was floored. "You're kicking your son out of his home? While he's in the middle of recovering from a dangerous accident? What kind of sick bastard are you?"

"I refuse to stand behind your godforsaken lifestyle. What you're doing is a sin."

"Loving someone is a sin?"

"Lying with another man is. Sodomy is."

"You know what, I'm going to let you go now. We'll be out of your house in thirty days. And don't worry about calling Luke until you've given up your bigoted ways."

Matt ended the call, but he was so infuriated, so completely pissed off, he growled and chucked the cordless phone across the yard. It bounced off the fence and hit the side of the house, shattering into tiny pieces. Zeus barked, chasing after the flying shards.

"Zeus!" Matt called, and the puppy came running.

When they went back inside, he found Luke staring at the frozen picture on the TV screen. He looked so damn relaxed. Matt hated the idea of telling him what that piece of shit father of his said. "Who was it?" he asked.

Matt watched Zeus run over to his little doggy bed. The pup walked circles, pawing at the bedding. He stopped, then started circling in the other direction. The animal served as a brief distraction, a reason for Matt not to immediately answer the question so he could think of how much he wanted to tell Luke.

"Matt?"

"It was your dad." Matt swung his gaze back around to the couch.

Frowning hard, Luke eased up from the bundle of blankets and pillows. "What the hell did he want?"

With a sigh, Matt sat down beside him. He brushed his thumb back and forth over his brow, then settled in for a discussion that would inevitably turn ugly. "Luke, your dad's an asshole," he said, leaning his elbow against his knees and clamping his hands together. "He wants us out of this house. Said we have thirty days." He caught Luke tensing out of the corner of his eye. That alone was enough to piss Matt off, but he let it go, because getting all riled up wouldn't benefit the situation one bit.

"So that's how he wants to play, huh?" Luke nodded a few too many times. He pulled his bottom lip between his teeth and bit down so hard the skin turned pale white.

"Luke…."

"No. No. He did this. He chose this. I'm done with him."

"Let's just sleep on this. We still have my house. I can move everything back in." Then there was the other option, the one Matt hadn't mentioned to Luke yet. He turned on the couch and laid his hand over Luke's. "Or… we could move up to New England. My brother wants me and Mom to move up that way. He wants me to work on the boat with him."

Closing his eyes, Luke sat back on the couch and pulled the blanket up to his chin. He didn't say anything immediately. For a moment, Matt thought he'd screwed up. He thought he'd pushed a little too hard and expected a little too much. Then Luke rolled his head to the side, looking right at Matt and said, "Screw it. Let's do it."

CHAPTER THIRTY-THREE

AT THE crack of dawn the next day, or close enough to be way too damn early, noise from the kitchen made Matt bolt straight up in the bed. He immediately thought someone had broken into the house, but the dog wasn't barking. He wasn't in the room like he had been when they'd all gone to bed the night before, but he wasn't raising hell either.

Matt eased out of bed, careful not to wake Luke—even though Luke slept like the dead—grabbed his robe, then tightened it around his body. He crept through the bedroom door, down the hallway, and into the living room where he found Zeus sitting on his haunches, tail wagging wildly along the hardwood floor. No intruder would've had Zeus's attention like that. That pup would've been raising hell.

Humming came from the kitchen. Matt recognized that tune, and the higher octave of his mother's voice. The song spilled from her soul when she was in the zone. She'd also sung it to him at bedtime as a child. It made sense for her to be there. She still had her key from when Luke was in the hospital so she could come over and take care of Zeus.

Matt let out the breath he'd been holding, then pressed on through the living room and over to the doorway leading into the kitchen. He leaned against the jamb, arms crossed over his chest. "I hope you made coffee."

"Brewing," she chimed before continuing with her song. Her elegant smile pushed dimples into her cheeks. Her salt-and-pepper hair was pulled up in a bun high atop her head. A red apron covered the front of her clothes.

"What are you doing here so early?"

"It's Thanksgiving. I'm cooking, remember?"

"Mom, it's not even—" He looked over his shoulder at the clock on the living room mantel. "—six in the morning."

"Well, I wanted to cook breakfast for my kiddos before I took over the kitchen."

"Looks like you've already taken over." Matt laughed. "I suppose that means I need to get Sleeping Beauty out of bed, then."

She made another high-pitched humming sound, still sorting plates and dumping food here and there. Matt hadn't woken up enough to really focus on everything, and just before he turned to head back to the bedroom, his mother said, "Not so fast, young man."

He looked back at her, and she had a tray in her hands. On top of it was a huge helping of scrambled eggs, a pile of toast, a mound of hash browns, and real bacon. She'd poured two glasses of OJ and two cups of coffee.

"Thank you," he said as he took the tray from her hands. He carefully leaned across it and kissed his mother's forehead. "I love you, Mom."

"I know, sweetie," she said as she reached up and patted his cheek. "I love you too."

Of all the things Matt was thankful for, his mother had to be at the top of that list. No matter what decisions he made throughout his life, she always stood by him. Even after he'd come out of the closet, she never raised her voice and never called him names. Granted, she didn't stand up to his dad on his behalf, but she never once turned her back on him. She never stopped loving him.

Using his foot, Matt opened the bedroom door a little wider so he could step through without knocking the tray out of his hands. The lights were still off, and he had to step carefully so he didn't spill the food. He set the tray down on the dresser, then went to the bed and turned the nightstand lamp on.

The light was enough for Matt to see Luke's peaceful, sleeping face. His lips held a slight smile, enough of a curve to show off Luke's dimples. The new moustache Matt thought he hated actually made Luke a little more debonair. The five-o'clock shadow gave him a hint of rugged rawness. The whole package was incredibly beautiful.

"Luke," Matt whispered as he reached down to cup his lover's face. He brushed his thumb over Luke's slightly parted lips. "Babe, time to wake up. Mom made breakfast for us." Luke's eyelids fluttered. "That's it. Let me see them pretty baby blues."

"What time is it?" Luke asked, voice gravelly.

"You don't want to know, I promise. Think you can sit up for me?"

"Yeah."

Luke winced as he eased up in the bed. Matt quickly reached across him for another pillow, then carefully tucked it behind Luke's back. The moment Luke settled in, his shoulders rounded and his expression softened.

Matt went back to the dresser and divvied out pills from each of Luke's many prescriptions and grabbed one of the glasses of OJ. He returned to Luke and patiently waited as his lover took each pill. Then he took the tray, folded out the legs, and set it across Luke's lap.

"Damn, your mom made a lot of food," Luke said.

"It's for both of us. Apparently, she's commandeering the kitchen for the day and wanted to make sure we had plenty of food so we wouldn't get in the way."

Luke laughed as Matt sat down beside him, and they each grabbed a fork.

They both dug in—alternating between shoveling food into their mouths and sucking down coffee. Not a single bite was left behind, and once they'd completely cleared the plates, Matt gathered the tray, then returned it to the kitchen. As miserably full as all the food made him, he still went right to cleaning up their dishes, but his mom stopped him.

"I'll handle the dishes," she said. "You just take care of Luke."

"He probably wants to take a bath. He didn't get one last night."

"Then what are you waiting for?" She stopped what she was doing, turned, arched her brow, and held up her forefinger, pointing it in Matt's direction. "But no hanky-panky."

Matt couldn't do anything more than laugh, but not in a condescending way. He shook his head, then went back to the bedroom where he found Luke rubbing his bloated stomach and staring at the blank TV screen. After the phone call from his father the night before, Luke had had more than a few of those quiet, distant moments. Matt would've given anything to take that misery away from the man he loved, but how could he?

"You wanna get a bath?" he asked as he made his way farther into the bedroom.

"I guess," Luke said with a shrug.

"Everything will be okay, I promise. Your dad will come around. If he doesn't, screw him. It's his loss. You still have people who love you."

"It's not him. It's my mom. I can't believe she's standing behind him and letting him do this to me."

Matt sat back down on the edge of the bed. He laid his hand on Luke's lower leg and said, "You remember how my mom reacted to my coming out?"

"You mean how she didn't react?"

"Yeah," Matt said. Luke nodded. "You see how she is now, right?"

"Yeah."

"Maybe your mom just doesn't want a confrontation. She does have to live with him, after all. Maybe she'll come around."

"Maybe."

"Come on," Matt said as he stood again. "Let's get you in the bath. I'm sure that'll help."

He handed Luke the robe hanging on the headboard, then reached for the crutches leaning against the wall and held them up for Luke to lift himself from the bed. The expression on Luke's face didn't change. He still looked completely depressed. Not that Matt could blame him. Having a parent disown him had to be hard as hell. Matt couldn't relate, but he could damn sure sympathize. His ex-sister-in-law had made life real damn miserable for him there for a while, and Matt had thought he might never see his brother again.

Walking close behind Luke, they both headed into the bathroom. Luke sat down on the toilet and removed the robe. Matt shrugged out of his, then hung them both on a wall hook close to the door. He filled the tub with hot water, then helped Luke up from the toilet.

Luke held on to him tight. "Thank you for hanging in there through all this shit. I know it's not easy, and you could probably stand to be anywhere else but here."

"No. There's nowhere else I'd rather be. I love you, and I love taking care of you."

"I love you too."

CHAPTER THIRTY-FOUR

MARK'S VOICE echoed through the house, followed by the sound of Matt's mom squealing and Emma's high-pitched giggles. Matt and Luke had been sitting in the living room on the couch with Zeus in between. The Thanksgiving Day parade played on the television, though neither of them really bothered watching it. They both had something on their minds. Matt knew what was on Luke's, but he would bet his life Luke didn't know what was on his.

"Little brother," Mark called from the doorway, arms spread wide.

Matt grinned and pushed up from the couch, pounded across the room, and met his brother in the tightest hug. They both slapped their meaty hands against each other's backs before pulling away.

"You remember Luke, right?" Matt asked.

"Of course," Mark said as he stepped up to the couch with his hand out for Luke to shake.

Luke said, "I would stand up, but…."

"No, man. Don't worry about it. Matt told me what happened to you. That had to be some pretty scary shit."

"You don't know the half of it. I saw the roof coming down, and I knew I was in trouble." As Luke told the story of what happened to him that day, Matt listened closely. He'd seen the aftermath but never thought to ask about the experience. "I hit the floor and curled my back up like I was trained. I thought everything would be fine, but the moment the roof hit the floor, it began to shake, and the next thing I knew, I was falling. When everything finally stopped moving, I hit the ground so hard I was pretty much spread-eagle. The roof came down with me, and that's all I remembered until I woke up in the hospital. I swear to God, I thought I died."

"Damn, bro," Mark said. Eyes wide, he sank down on the chair across from Luke. Matt leaned against the doorway. "You plan on going back to fighting fires?"

Wouldn't we all like to know?

As if Luke read Matt's thoughts, he raised his head and met Matt's curious stare. He said, "If they tell me I can, I might. Looks like I might be transferring stations, though."

"Oh yeah?" Mark asked.

"Yeah," Luke said, still staring at Matt. "Somewhere up in New England from what I understand."

Mark's eyes widened. His head whipped back and forth as his stare ping-ponged between Luke and Matt. Matt couldn't tell if Mark believed them or if he was excited about it or freaked or… or anything.

"Mark, will you say something?" Matt asked.

"Hell yeah, I'll say something. I'm freakin' stoked, bro. I'm glad you finally decided to move up there."

"Well, the decision was…." Matt's voice trailed off. He wasn't sure if he needed to share the crap Luke's father had pulled with them.

"The best one we could've made," Luke finished for him.

He gave Matt a look, and what Matt saw was a willingness to do whatever it took to make their relationship work. He knew then that Luke would stand by his side no matter what. Their friendship had always been strong, damn strong, and Matt knew beyond a shadow of a doubt, as a couple, they would survive anything.

And in that split second of realization, that's when Matt made the smartest decision he ever had. "Can you give me a second?" he asked as he pushed up from the wall.

Every stare in the room followed him as he hurried down the hall and back to the bedroom they'd been sharing since Luke came home from the hospital. He flipped on the lights and quickly scoured the room for his trusty old duffel bag, the one that held the very important keepsake box he'd been hanging on to since high school.

The bag was on the floor by the chair. He sat down and started to dig through it until he found the small wooden chest. For a moment, he gripped both edges and thought about what he was about to do.

The ring inside that box hadn't been bought for Luke, but part of Matt knew the reason he never gave it to Brandon was because it'd been meant for someone else, someone who'd never failed him, who he'd always loved and considered his other half long before Brandon had ever come into the picture. Luke was the reason no other man would ever have his heart, and it only made sense for Matt to vow to spend his life with Luke.

Yes. This was the right decision.

He pulled the velvety box out of the chest, opened it, and took one of the titanium bands off the display. Curling his fingers around the ring, he set the chest back down on the chair and smiled. This was the best decision he could've made. Even if Luke turned him down, he would still vow to love, honor, and cherish that man forever and always.

Matt hurried back into the living room. Luke frowned in his direction. Mark arched his brow. Matt smiled wildly and said, "Mom. Emma. Come here for a second."

"Bro, what's up?" Mark asked cautiously.

Matt didn't say a word.

The women entered the room, stopping at the doorway where Matt had once been standing. "What's wrong?" his mother asked.

"Nothing," Matt said with a smile. "Nothing at all."

The moment he knelt down in front of Luke, he heard someone gasp behind him, but that didn't stop him. It didn't even slow him down. Holding the ring between the thumb and forefinger of one hand, he reached for Luke's curled fist, stared up at his lover's beautiful, crystal blue eyes, and said, "We've had a long relationship that's survived so much, and I know being with me is new to you. I know being in *this* kind of relationship is new to you, but I would be honored if you would consider marrying me. I love you, Luke. Always have and always will. And I want you to be the only person I ever sleep beside, laugh with, and live with. I want you to know you're the only person I'll ever truly love."

"Matt, I...."

Luke sat there staring—eyes wide, mouth agape. Matt heard someone sniffling behind him, and while he wanted to look for approving gazes, he didn't want to take his eyes off the man he was ready to commit his life to. Matt clenched his jaw and pinched his lips shut, waiting for what would hopefully come out as an excited "yes." Every second of silence made him a little more nervous. If Luke turned him down….

"Yes," Luke finally said. "Yes."

The breath that darted out of Matt's body seemed to be the only thing keeping him so solid, because when he let it go, his broad chest deflated, and his square shoulders rounded. He laid his head in Luke's lap and closed his eyes, whispering a relieved, "Thank God."

"Just so you know," Mark chimed in, "same-sex marriage isn't a big deal in Connecticut. Nobody's gonna try to stop you there."

CHAPTER THIRTY-FIVE

"WE SHOULD have a summer wedding, by a lake," Matt's mom said as she carried empty plates over to the sink. Emma washed the dishes as Mom handed them to her. Every single soul at the kitchen table rubbed their stomachs. "Don't you think a summer wedding would be beautiful?"

"Mom," Matt sighed.

"We could have it at Mark's house. There's a small lake at the back of his property," Emma offered.

"Sure is," Mark said.

"Mark!" Matt said.

"What?" Mark shrugged.

Luke only laughed and shook his head. He so wasn't helping.

"Can you guys calm down?" Matt asked. "There's no need to rush us off to the altar. We have time. Plus, we have some things to deal with here. I need to get my house sold, and if we're sincerely going to move up north, we need to find a place there."

"If you guys want to rent the apartment above the bar, you can," Emma offered.

Matt frowned and turned in his chair. "What about you? Where are you going to live?"

Mark cleared his throat and quickly looked away. Every head in the room turned his way. He rubbed his thumb and forefinger over his eyes and said, "I guess we should share our big news with 'em, huh?"

Emma nodded slowly.

Matt sat back in his chair and crossed his arms over his chest as a devious grin curled the edges of his lips. Oh, he couldn't wait to hear this. His big brother, Mr. I'm-Done-With-Women, was moving his girlfriend in with him.

"We're having a baby," Mark confessed.

Well, Matt never saw *that* news coming.

"A baby!" their mother squealed. She immediately threw her arms around Emma's neck. Poor Emma had nowhere to run before the hugging and kissing started. She was trapped between their mother and the sink. "A baby," their mother sighed happily. "How far along are you? Couldn't be far. You're as skinny as a rail."

"About a month and a half," Emma said.

"A baby," Momma Murphy said for the third time as she cradled Emma's face between her hands. Matt and Mark exchanged glances. Mark just shook his head. Their mother loved kids, loved babies even more… loved spoiling the babies. Before that kid ever entered the world, it would have anything and everything it could possibly need for the next few years of its life.

"So, about moving up north, Mom," Mark said. "Looks like you're gonna have more than one reason to go."

"Yeah, Mom," Matt chimed in as he wrapped his fingers around Luke's. "We'll all be there. You'll love Connecticut, anyways. It's gorgeous."

"I don't want to sell the house," she finally admitted. "Your father and I bought that house right after we got married. We've put every single dime we had into it."

"You're not even living in the house right now, Ma," Matt said.

"That's not the point. You'll understand after the two of you buy your first house. It's a hard thing to get rid of."

"What about renting it out?" Luke offered.

"We would have to fix it up," she said.

"That's what Mark and I are for, Ma. We'll get it fixed up, and you can find a local realtor to manage it for you."

It was a perfect plan, everyone agreed, even their mother. The entire family was destined to relocate up to New England so they could all be together again. Matt now had the love of his life and had a new niece or nephew to look forward to. Everything was perfect again. Well, almost everything.

Luke kept a smile on his face, but there was something dark and distant in the way he stared at the wall or maybe the window. Matt didn't have to ask what was wrong. He already knew. They all sat around rejoicing and celebrating their happiness and togetherness, and Luke's parents had pretty much disowned him. He couldn't call them and tell them Matt had proposed. They didn't want to hear about it and damn sure wouldn't be happy about it, and sadly, that wasn't fair to Luke.

Matt brushed his thumb over Luke's knuckles as he leaned in and rested his arm along the back of Luke's chair. It took Matt pressing a chaste kiss to his temple before Luke finally turned his stare back to Matt. "You look tired. You wanna go to bed?" Matt whispered while everyone around them continued to plan their new bright and shiny future together.

"I don't want to be a buzzkill," Luke said.

"You won't be. They'll understand. And I'll stay back there with you."

"And miss out on time with your family? Don't do that on my account."

"Sounds like we'll have plenty of time with them soon enough." Matt looked back up at his mom and cleared his throat. All conversation instantly ceased. "I'm going to take Luke to bed, okay? You guys don't give Zeus any table scraps, and lock up when you leave, please?"

"We'll handle everything, sweetie," his mom said as she poured another cup of coffee. She came over to the table, kissed Luke on the crown of his head, then Matt. She said to her son, "You take care of my new son. Ya hear me?"

"Yes, ma'am," Matt said as he reached for Luke's crutches.

He helped Luke—his fiancé—back to the bedroom and into the bed, then leaned the crutches against the wall. He didn't offer to take off Luke's T-shirt and sweatpants. In fact, he opted to keep himself dressed as well. Now felt like the time to cuddle and coddle, not for steamy liaisons and unyielding desires.

Matt climbed into the bed next to Luke, laid his arm across his lover's stomach and his head on Luke's chest. "I'm sorry you had to deal with all that happy family stuff. I know it had to be hard," he offered, gently brushing the tips of his fingers over the spot above Luke's heart.

"No. Don't apologize for that. It was nice to be a part of it. I just wished my own parents would come around."

"Don't give up hope, okay? Things change. People change."

"My father hasn't changed in the thirty-five years I've known him. I knew this would happen. That's why I never let my sexuality come out. That's why I kept it a secret even from you."

"Well, I'm personally glad you finally came out to me. I can't even begin to describe how happy I am that we finally have a chance to be together."

"You don't have to," Luke said softly as he pressed his lips to the crown of Matt's head. "It shows in the way you look at me and hold me, in everything you do for me."

The conversation died down. Matt never moved from Luke's chest, and Luke never once complained. Eventually, they both fell asleep—stomachs full and hearts as content as they could be. Nothing was perfect, and that was okay. The world wasn't a perfect place, but they had each other, and at least one side of the family supported them and loved them both unconditionally. That alone gave them reason to celebrate. That alone gave them all the happiness they needed—bigoted fathers be damned.

CHAPTER THIRTY-SIX

IT WAS entirely too damn cold outside to try to work on his mother's house, but despite being able to see every single breath they took and the chill numbing their fingers, Matt and Mark took to doing what they did best—fix shit.

Well, Matt had a lot more talent than his brother in that respect, but Mark followed directions well. Even Luke helped as much as he could. He handled the table saw, cut all the pieces to keep the job flowing along. They'd found a stool just tall enough for Luke to reach the table with no problems.

Their mom and Emma worked on what they could inside, mostly sweeping and cleaning, since paint fumes were bad for Emma and the baby. When it came time to take a short break, they joined the boys outside.

"And the first time Mark broke his arm," Matt heard his mother saying. He lifted his head to catch her pointing at a tree in the front yard, with her other arm wrapped around Emma's waist. "He had this tire swing."

"Whoa," Mark said, "C'mon, Ma. If you're gonna tell the story, tell it right. That stupid swing belonged to Matty."

"And Mark wouldn't let me swing on it. He kept pushing me off of it," Matt piped up.

"Lies. All lies," Mark said.

"Well regardless," their mother interrupted. "The tree limb broke and landed on Mark's arm, fractured it in two places."

"That's because his fat ass shouldn't have been on the damn swing in the first place," Matt mumbled.

Mark tossed a two-by-two chunk of wood at Matt's feet, and Matt jumped in just enough time not to get hit. He chuckled. Mark swore under his breath. Emma and Luke both laughed. Their mother said, "Y'all aren't too old to have your fannies whipped."

The laughter only grew louder from that point, until a car pulling up to the curb stole everyone's attention. Behind the wheel was a beautiful fair-haired woman in a bright red coat and a scarf tied up to her chin. Sunglasses hid her eyes, even with the dreary gray of the December afternoon sky looming overhead. Matt didn't need to see her eyes anyway. He knew exactly who it was when he saw the car.

The hammer slid out of his hand as he stepped closer to Luke. His muscles tensed, and his breath caught in his throat. He kept his stare on the woman, watching her like a hawk as she climbed out of the car.

"No," Luke gasped softly.

"It's okay," Matt offered, reaching down for his lover's hand.

"Who is that?" Mark asked.

"Luke's mom," their mother bitterly replied.

A wall of bodies formed beside Luke, starting with Matt who still held his hand, then their mother, with Mark and Emma capping off the end. They were all like a well-oiled machine, ready to stand guard to protect Luke from the people who'd hurt him.

Mrs. Bishop's heels clicked against the paved sidewalk as she so carefully made her way up to the house. She avoided eye contact with everyone but Luke, while everyone but Luke stared at her like she was the devil incarnate.

The truth about how Luke's family had treated him after they'd found Matt kneeling at his feet at the hospital had come out only a few nights ago. No one had really had much of a chance to get over their shock, partly because Luke had confessed the truth of his parents' bigotry out of the blue. No rhyme or reason, just a blatant, "They hate me," like it was a sudden realization. It had spawned a three-hour conversation.

"What do you want?" Matt barked.

"I want to talk to my son," Mrs. Bishop immediately responded.

Matt opened his mouth to speak, but the moment he did, he felt Luke's fingers tighten around his. Apparently, Luke didn't need or want anyone standing up for him.

162

"Then talk," Luke barked. His voice trembled only slightly. Matt wasn't sure if the quiver came from anger or hurt.

"Luke, we need to talk… privately," she said.

"No, we don't. They all know what you and Dad did to me, what you said, and how you kicked me out of my home. Nothing is a secret, and they're all my family now. So whatever you need to say, you can say it in front of them too."

"Maybe we should give them some privacy," Matt heard his mother whisper. He could tell by the direction of her voice she'd said the words more to Emma and Mark as opposed to him. She wouldn't say something like that to him anyway. Anything involving Luke involved him as well.

The three of them—Mark, Emma, and their mother—left Luke and Matt standing outside with Mrs. Bishop. Though it seemed like a bit of tension eased away, no one acted as if they wanted to be the first one to break the silence.

"This is ridiculous," Matt finally said. "If you want to say something, say it. Otherwise, we're all standing around freezing for no good reason."

"I'm sorry," Mrs. Bishop said. She'd had her eyes on Luke, but slowly turned toward Matt. "To both of you, I'm sorry. I didn't agree with anything Luke's father said, but I couldn't make myself speak up."

"Then why are you here now?" Luke asked, keeping his jaw clenched tightly. Obviously so he wouldn't raise his voice.

"Because I didn't want you to think I hated you or thought ill of you. I didn't want Matt thinking I was angry at him. I love you, both of you, and if you're happy together, then I'm happy for you."

"Did you tell Dad that?"

She shifted her eyes, as if she didn't dare to look directly at her son. "Not yet" was what she finally said, though Matt had a feeling it wasn't 100 percent truth.

"Will you?"

"I don't know, Lucas."

Tell him the truth, Matt thought. *Whatever the truth is, just tell him.*

Luke licked his lips and lowered his head. He flexed his fist, opened and closed, around Matt's hand. Matt watched the slow, deliberate rise and fall of his lover's chest, as if Luke were trying to take deep, even breaths just to remain calm. When he spoke again, he kept his head bowed. "Then it sounds like to me you have nothing to offer me but empty words, and I'm not interested."

God, Matt had no clue Luke could be so cold. Not that his mother didn't deserve it, but holy shit. Who knew mild-mannered Luke had it in him? Matt would've hated to be in her shoes at the moment.

His mother lifted her chin and all but glared down the line of her nose. "If that's how you feel...."

"It is."

"I understand."

Mrs. Bishop turned to walk away, only the chin she'd once held so high dropped a little lower. Her gait slowed considerably, as if she'd lost all that steely confidence she'd had when she first arrived. They couldn't see her face, but Matt imagined there being real sorrow in her eyes. He thought everything was said and done, but then Luke called out to her, "We're getting married." The woman stopped dead in her tracks. She didn't turn around but didn't take another step. "And we're moving away to New England... in case you wanted to know."

Why Luke decided to tell her those facts the way he did, Matt didn't know. Maybe it was a jab just for the sake of making her hurt a little more. Whatever, Luke obviously had his reasons, reasons he may or may not share with Matt one day, but Matt wouldn't ask.

"I think we should call it a night," Matt quietly suggested.

"No." Luke spun back around on the stool. "I want to keep working."

The kind of determination he saw in Luke couldn't be argued with, and Matt didn't want to start a fight. So he let his lover keep on truckin', sawing away at the bits of wood. Matt shook his head, then went back up to the house. The moment he stepped inside, everyone rushed him. They all wanted to know what happened, if Luke was okay, what he said.

"Can we please just get back to work?" Matt asked, tone laced with exasperation.

"It's getting late, though," Matt's mom said.

"Yeah, but Luke doesn't want to stop. So, can we just go out there with him or… something?"

"How about I take Emma home with me," his mom offered, "and you two can stay with Luke?"

"That sounds like a good plan."

Mark leaned down to give Emma a quick kiss, then hugged his mom. Matt hugged the ladies as well. They walked out the door first, and the guys followed. They found Luke still plugging away at the wood he'd been cutting. He didn't so much as raise his head. Not until the whizzing of the saw quieted and Luke righted himself. Matt's mom touched the middle of his back and said, "You take it easy out here. We want to get you in tip-top shape so you can walk down the aisle with my son." Luke only nodded.

He waited for the women to leave, waited for Mark to pick his hammer back up, and then he went over to Luke and laid his hand on the nape of Luke's bowed neck. "Talk to me," Matt said, and the moment the words left his lips, Luke threw his arms around Matt's neck and started to cry in a way Matt had never seen before.

No words were spoken about Luke's tears. Nothing needed to be said. Matt knew what was going on, and he knew Luke just needed to cry it out. What he'd said to his mom took a hell of a lot of guts. Whether it was the right thing to say or the wrong thing didn't matter. It broke him in a way Matt could understand, and Matt would be the one to help him heal from those wounds.

CHAPTER THIRTY-SEVEN

"LOOKS LIKE you might get a white Christmas after all, Mom," Matt called from the sunroom of his new Connecticut home. The wall of windows in front of him faced a dense forest that led to God only knew where. He hadn't been brave enough to wander out there yet. "The snow's already collecting on the pines."

"Really?" she yelled from the kitchen. "Stay right there. I'm coming to see it."

Matt laughed and shook his head, then took his spot right next to Zeus and Luke on the lounger. They'd been cuddling there for the better half of the afternoon, watching TV and waiting for the snow the weatherman promised while Matt's mother tooled around in the kitchen. From the smell of it, making every baked good she could think of for Mark's Christmas celebration with the crew.

Her tiny fuzzy-socked footfalls rapidly thumped across the kitchen tiles, then onto the hardwood. There, in the sunroom, with that veil of white light glowing from the windows, his mother stopped in her tracks. Her eyes widened, and her mouth gaped. At home in Tennessee, a white Christmas was a song on the radio, not a tradition. They hadn't seen genuine snow that thick—not ice and sludge—since Matt and Mark were young boys.

"It's beautiful," she breathed.

"It really is," Luke said with a dreamy-eyed smile.

Matt tightened his arms around Luke's body and held him against his chest. The warmth radiating from his lover was better than any kind of manufactured heat, and suddenly Matt found himself thinking like one of those hopelessly romantic saps the old black-and-white movies were made of.

"I should get back to cooking," his mom said.

"Do you want some help?" Matt asked.

"Honey, no offense, but I've seen you in the kitchen, and I don't have time for any disasters."

Everyone in the room laughed. Hell, even Zeus raised his head and snorted out a little sound. "Fine," Matt said playfully. "I didn't want to get up anyway."

About that time, he heard the squeaking hinges of the side door, then the slam, and his brother's voice asking "Is anyone here?"

Well, duh! Surely the genius saw the cars and motorcycle. Surely he smelled their mother's cooking, and he had to have heard the damn TV. People in New Mexico could probably hear the TV.

"In the sunroom," Matt called over his shoulder.

His flannel-clad older brother stepped to the doorway first. Emma stood sort of behind, sort of to the side of him, but beyond them all was someone much shorter, with a head full of blonde hair. Matt's stomach instantly knotted, and he glared up at his brother.

"What the hell is going on here?" he demanded as he popped up from the couch. Zeus jumped down to the floor. Luke's head whipped back. "What the hell is she doing here?"

"Matty, listen for a minute," his mother said. She held up both hands. "I know you had words last time y'all saw each other, but we talked, and you need to hear her out."

"I don't want to 'hear her out'!" Matt declared.

"Young man," his mom said, voice turning stern like it used to when he was a kid and got in trouble for being a jackass. She pointed her momma finger at his sternum. "I raised you better than this. Now, you're going to sit down and act like you got some sense, 'kay? Okay. Good."

Matt sat down beside Luke, clenching his jaw so tight it was a wonder his teeth didn't combust inside his mouth. Frankly, he didn't give a shit what Mrs. Bishop had to say.

"C'mon," Matt's mom said, wrapping her arms around Mark and Emma. "Let's give 'em some space."

His mom walked them both out of the room. She gave Mrs. Bishop a look in passing, the same kind of look she'd given Matt when she wanted to convince him something was completely safe to do but didn't want to seem too prodding. Mrs. Bishop cautiously stepped through the door.

In all his demanding and insisting they didn't want to see her, Matt hadn't taken Luke's feelings on the matter into consideration. Shameful but true. He just assumed Luke didn't want to see his mom after the altercation back in Tennessee. But the moment she stepped into Luke's direct line of sight, something in his expression softened. There was no anger there, no silent dismissal of her presence. Matt saw something resembling curiosity and maybe even a hint of need. Maybe Luke did genuinely *need* his mother to accept him.

"What made you decide to come all the way up here?" Luke finally said as he sat up on the couch next to Matt. He leaned forward—steepling his elbows against his knees, hands locked beneath his chin. He appeared to be looking at his mother, but Matt couldn't tell for sure.

"Because, there were things I wanted to say to you in Memphis," she said, "but I wasn't really given much of a chance."

Luke nodded toward a chair that matched the lounger they'd been nestled on half the day. "Well, sit down and talk. Here's your chance to say whatever's on your mind. Matt and I will keep our mouths shut until you're finished."

She tightened her coat around her body and settled into the chair—shoulders squared, knees pressed tight together, hands folded in her lap like a genuine lady. As far as Matt was concerned, looks could be deceiving.

"I can't stand behind your father anymore, Luke," she cautiously began. "I don't agree with the way he treated you. When he called to kick you out of the house, I told him not to, or I would leave him. He didn't believe I would do it. I did. I just needed time to find a new home so I could get out of there. I'm divorcing him."

"You are?" Luke asked, voice airy with surprise.

"I had the papers drawn the day I stopped by to visit you."

They both stared at Mrs. Bishop with their mouths agape. Matt couldn't believe his ears, and now he felt like shit for being so rude to her before. If she just would've said something, Matt would've kept his mouth shut, and things could've worked out so much differently.

Her eyes started turning glassy. She fidgeted with her fingers, knuckles turning white every time she wrung her hands. Luke stood from the couch and took a few steps, and his mother stood to meet him halfway. They met in a hug, and she buried her face against Luke's sweatshirt. He cradled the back of her head with his thick, strong hand. Matt didn't know what to do. He felt completely out of place, like an outsider watching a heartfelt reunion.

"Why didn't you tell me?" Luke whispered. "Why didn't you say something that day?"

"I don't know. It didn't feel right. I wanted to, but I just… I couldn't do it." She looked up at him, and the rims of her eyes were bright red, lashes coated with tears. Her rosy cheeks had turned blotchy and the tip of her nose a rich pink. "I love you so much, Luke. There's no one in the world who will ever change that, not even your father. Who you love is who you love. As long as you're happy, I'm happy."

"You don't know how good it is to hear you say that. I never wanted to lose you, but I was so hurt. I thought I disappointed you."

"Never."

"I know that now. I'm so sorry for how I acted."

"Don't apologize, Luke. I should've been stronger. I should've stood behind you."

"You're here now. That's what matters to me."

Matt quietly stood from the couch with the hopes of ducking out of the room so they could have their mother-son moment, but the springs of the lounger betrayed him and sounded out a squeaky alert that made them both look his way.

"Sorry," he mouthed. "I was just going to let you guys have some privacy."

"No," Mrs. Bishop said as she held out her slender hand, fingers slightly curled in offering. He cautiously took her hand. "This is your business too, and I owe you an apology as well."

"Yeah, well, I guess we can all take a spot in the 'I'm sorry' line. I wasn't exactly warm to you either."

"Then how about mutual forgiveness?"

"Sounds good to me."

Matt brushed his fingers through the fallen locks of his wavy brown hair. His stare shifted back and forth across the room, looking for a quick escape. The only way he was getting out of that cramped room was to plow his way between Luke and his mother. He wouldn't do that, not even on a dare.

"Where are you staying?" Luke asked his mother.

"In a hotel not far from here. I wanted to spend Christmas with my son and his fiancé."

Frankly, Matt couldn't believe his ears. It started feeling like he'd somehow stepped into an alternate reality, or maybe aliens had abducted Luke's real mother. He opened his mouth, but didn't have a clue what to say. Part of him wanted to invite her to stay in the spare room while the other part wanted to ask her when she'd be heading far away from them.

"You could stay here," Luke offered. The words prompted Matt to finally exhale, then close his gaping mouth.

"I don't want to impose," she said.

"It's no imposition. We would love to have you," Matt added, even if the sentiment wasn't exactly true. He said it for Luke.

"If you're certain," Mrs. Bishop said. A grateful smile curled the edges of her lips.

"We're certain, Mom," Luke said. "Mrs. Murphy lives with Matt's brother, so she has a place already. I really don't want you staying in a hotel alone."

"It's settled, then," Matt said, clapping his hands together. "I'll get the spare room ready for her."

"Thank you, both of you. Thanks for having me."

Matt immediately took that as his cue to make an exit. Now he had a reason to bolt and thankfully, needing to straighten up the spare room would keep him from looking rude. He was happy Luke's mom seemed so open to the idea of them being together, but it was still a very weird situation for him. After all, he had gone the hell off on her and spent close to a month despising her. It took more than a few kind words to take such strong feelings away.

He pushed through the sunroom door and into the kitchen where his family stood waiting. They made failed attempts to hide their eavesdropping, but Matt didn't say anything about it. He just kept walking as if he didn't notice, and no one bothered to say a word. They kept on with what they were doing—or rather, what they wanted it to *look* like they were doing.

Back in the spare room, he grabbed a change of linens from the closet and took to changing the bed. Thankfully, they'd managed to get everything unpacked and put away, so the spare boxes they'd stashed in that room were gone, save for a few stragglers.

Matt unfolded the fitted sheet, snapped it out and stretched it across the bed. He settled each corner, then went to the next sheet. Knocking on the door gave him a start, and the linen slipped from his hand, then flittered down to the floor. He muttered curses beneath his breath as he reached down to get it. "Come in," he called over his shoulder.

"You sure you're okay with Mom staying here?" Luke asked.

The question made Matt freeze where he stood. "Yeah. I'm fine."

"You don't seem fine," Luke said as he reached for the other corner of the sheet. "In fact, you seem a little irritated."

"I'm not. I promise. I'm just... uncomfortable."

"Why?"

"Man, do you not remember how I talked to her? People don't forget that kind of disrespect. She might put on a happy face for you, but there's no way she's forgiven me for talking to her the way I did."

"Maybe not, but I'm sure she understands."

"Maybe," Matt said with a shrug. He went back to making the bed.

CHAPTER THIRTY-EIGHT

THE NIGHT wound down quickly after the dinner Matt's mom had made. It was some kind of rice and chicken dish, with baked bread and steamed veggies. Matt missed his mom's cooking, though she lived close enough for him to have dinner with her every night. Life happened and time flew, and before he knew it, Matt'd missed a week's worth of opportunities with her. The cycle continued.

As the hours passed, he'd become slightly more comfortable with Mrs. Bishop's presence, especially after the shared stories of their teenage years and the antics Luke and Matt used to get into. The laughter in the room had been a blessing, one Matt felt incredibly thankful for as soon as he'd seen the way Luke's face had lit up.

That little reunion seemed to be a win for everyone.

Mrs. Bishop hugged Luke and Matt good night. She told them not to wait up, that she needed to go to the hotel and pick up her things. The drive back wasn't the shortest.

MATT SETTLED into the bed, blankets pulled up over his bare chest. The fleece felt amazing against his skin, but not half as amazing as Luke's touch. Luke was still lounging in the oversized bathtub. He spent hours in there sometimes, especially when his back really started to bother him. After making the bed for Mrs. Bishop, Luke started complaining about it hurting, and despite the intense massage Matt had given him after dinner and conversation with their family, Luke still needed to soak in the heat.

The bathroom door opened. Light and steam poured into their dim bedroom, haloing Luke's beautifully toned body. He held a towel to his navel, and it blocked the view. "You look comfy," he said softly.

"I am. I'd be more comfy if you were in the bed with me."

172

"Oh, I'm on my way, I promise."

Luke dropped the towel and exposed his soft shaft. Even without it being hard, it impressed the hell out of Matt. Or maybe that had more to do with the fact he loved that man so much and finally being able to lie naked beside him was a dream come true, a dream Matt never in a million years thought would become reality.

He pulled the sheets back, offering Luke a spot to climb in. Luke's stare immediately landed on Matt's completely naked, completely exposed body. Matt reached down between his legs and wrapped his hand over his crotch. The base of his shaft nestled into the bend of his thumb and forefinger. He kept his gaze on Luke. "We haven't made love yet… save for me giving you a blowjob or two, but I don't really consider that the same. Do you?"

"I don't," Luke said breathlessly.

"Then climb into bed with me, please."

As Luke crossed the room—muscles flexing, cock stirring, Matt kept his eyes trained on his lover. Of all the men Matt had been with, Luke was the complete package—smart, gorgeous, funny, and caring. Luke was his best friend and the best person for Matt to spend the rest of his life with. He felt so stupid for ever trying to deny his feelings, for fighting the love he'd always felt just so he could be with someone else. He would never make that mistake again. Ever.

The mattress dipped as Luke lifted one knee and climbed into the bed next to Matt. His tan skin still had a glistening sheen from the moisture of the bath he'd soaked in, made more brilliant by the soft light of the lamp next to their bed. Matt laid his hand on the small of Luke's back, just beneath the pink sliver of scar where the doctors had sliced into his body to repair the damage of his fall. They'd come so close to losing each other forever. The scar reminded them both that life was too short not to be true to themselves, and they planned on living out their years together being exactly what they were meant to be from the very beginning of their relationship—lovers and friends.

He guided Luke down to the bed until Luke lay on his stomach. Matt lifted up onto all fours, hovering over Luke's body. He pressed his lips to one of his lover's shoulders as he rubbed his hand over the base of Luke's spine—massaging slowly, listening to every single satisfied moan that left the luscious curve of Luke's slightly parted lips.

Every sensual sound made Matt want to bury himself inside Luke's body, stroke and fondle and make love until they both came, then do it all over again. He had to stifle his desire with silent reminders of how gentle he needed to be with Luke right now. Not only because of the injury Luke had sustained, but he also didn't know how much experience Luke had when it came to sex.

He trailed kisses down Luke's back, slowly winding down the line of his spine until he reached the curve where his delectable ass met his waist. Matt let his lips linger there for a moment, gauging Luke's response—the moans and eager breaths, the way Luke seemed to curl his back only slightly. It all felt like a damn good indication for Matt to keep going.

So he did. He pressed his tongue to the top of the part between Luke's wonderfully rounded cheeks, then licked down the valley and over Luke's puckered rosette. Matt closed his eyes and circled his tongue around Luke's opening—once, twice, again and again, and with each pass, Luke's moans grew deeper, louder, more needing.

Easing his hand between the mattress and Luke's body, Matt let his fingertips glide over Luke's skin until he reached his lover's sac. He let his palm gently travel over the sensitive flesh until he had Luke cradled in his hand, and he caressed those two orbs as he licked across the valley of Luke's ass.

"God, that feels amazing," Luke breathed, and though he wouldn't have seen it, the words brought a smile to Matt's face. He absolutely loved how incredibly wanting Luke sounded, loved the way Luke's shaft hardened and thickened against his palm. It was a huge stroke to his ego, just knowing he could turn his lover on the way he had.

He lifted back up and said, "Let me get the lube." Because God knew, they would need it.

As he lifted up from the bed, he saw Luke turn his head to the side. He watched Matt—well, they watched each other closely, almost as if neither one of them wanted that incredibly sensual moment to end. But it wasn't truly ending. It was just beginning.

Matt reached in the nightstand drawer and fished around until he found the bottle of lube they had yet to break open. He peeled the little plastic seal away, popped the cap open, then squeezed a generous helping onto his hand.

Luke licked his lips. His eyes became hooded with the unmistakable weight of desire. He reached down beneath his body, and Matt could tell by the expression on his face and the flex of his muscled arm he'd wrapped his hand around his cock.

Matt did the same to his own, dragging the lube down his shaft, coating it until it was slick enough for Luke's body. He kept stroking, even as he climbed his way back up the bed. His rhythm didn't change, didn't falter nor rush.

"I love you," he whispered at the nape of Luke's neck as his slick, hardened cock pressed against the valley of his lover's ass. He ground himself against Luke's body, letting the warmth stroke him and keep him hard.

"I love you too," Luke said in an airy rush. He arched his back, pressing himself tighter against the expanse of Matt's body. "I feel like I've waited for this moment forever and now…."

"You can't believe we're finally here?"

"No, I can't."

"Me either."

"Then what are you waiting for?" Luke asked, peering over his shoulder.

Matt lifted his hips, angled his cock, then gently pressed the tip to Luke's puckered opening. He closed his eyes as he eased the head of his shaft inside Luke's tight warmth.

The hiss spilling from Luke's lips made Matt want to retreat. He silently reminded himself that Luke was very new to all of this, and a hiss was to be expected, as well as the clenching and the groaning.

"Relax for me," he said. "Just breathe and relax. I'll be gentle."

He didn't move another inch until he felt Luke relax, and once he felt confident in his lover's comfort, he continued slowly slipping more of his cock into Luke's body. The ring of muscle gripped his erection. Matt took it slow, letting the lube do its job. His slick cock dipped deeper into Luke's channel. After he was all the way in, buried to the hilt, he started pulling back again.

"You okay?" he asked.

Luke moaned as he nodded against the pillow.

Eventually, Matt found his rhythm. He kept the pace slow and steady, only picking up speed as Luke's body allowed him to. One palm pressed to the mattress beneath them, holding his weight so it didn't bear down on Luke's delicate spine. He reached around and wrapped the other around his lover's erection, pleased to find a silky droplet clinging to the head of Luke's cock. He started to stroke, kissing the back of Luke's neck as he rolled his hips.

The pleased, eager sounds of Luke's satisfaction gave Matt a new zeal. His pace quickened, both the kissing and the stroking, the way he made love to the only man who'd ever really touched his heart.

The next time he rolled his hips, dipping deep into Luke's warmth, his shaft rode over Luke's special spot, and a roar unlike anything Matt had ever heard rumbled through Luke's body. His lover growled into the pillow, and that's when Matt felt a burst of moist heat roll down between his fingers. He'd made Luke come, and that alone made Matt so incredibly proud of his prowess. It excited him.

He'd finally made love to the one man he'd ever really lusted for, dreamed of, and desired but thought he could never have. After twenty years of friendship, of laughs and tears, of fears and the happiest moments they both thought they would ever have, he'd finally shared the last thing he had left to share. He'd shared his love and his body.

EPILOGUE

MATT PACED back and forth, back and forth, wringing his hands and occasionally stealing a glance through the window overlooking his brother's property. Everything was on track, and his worry was completely unfounded. Between his and Luke's mothers, his brother and Emma, the wedding didn't have a chance in hell of falling apart, but Matt wouldn't calm down until he had Luke standing beside him at the altar, speaking the vows they'd worked so hard to perfect.

"You're wearing me out, dude," his brother said flatly, and the sound of Mark's voice gave him a start.

Raggedly exhaling, Matt slowly turned around and found Mark sitting on the edge of the bed, slipping his massive foot into a dress sock.

"I can't help it," Matt said. "We're not out of the woods yet. Everything can fall apart in the last minute. I mean, what if Luke backs out?"

Mark snorted. "You're insane, little bro. He ain't backing out. You two could've easily been on that show… what's it called, *Bridezillas* or something like that?"

"Bite me," Matt said turning back to the window.

He saw his mother talking to the judge. She had a smile on her face, which gave Matt only a modicum of calm. He still had the sweaty palms and shaky fingers, though, still had the thumping in his temples.

She guided the judge down the aisle, past the rows of white folding chairs capped on each end with a spray of calla lilies and bright green fronds, toward the altar near the little lake at the edge of Mark's property. They disappeared beneath a canopy of thick, green trees. He sighed, shoulders slumping, then turned back to his brother to tell him… something.

The sound of a thick, meaty fist banging on the door stole his thought. Again, Matt was so on edge the sudden pounding nearly made him jump out of his damn skin. "It's time, greenhorn," Scotty called through the wooden surface. "Y'all better come on. I wanna getcha married before Christmas. And I wanna get outta dis damn suit."

"Calm down," Mark said. "We're comin'."

"Ay, Captain."

Mark stood from the bed, and he laid his heavy hand on Matt's shoulder. They exchanged a quick look. "You ready for this? You ready to take the plunge, to have your ball and chain, to lose your freedom, to—"

"Stop. Please. God. Stop. I'm already nervous as hell."

"I know, and I think it's hilarious." Mark winked. "Consider it payback for what you did to me on my wedding day."

"Yeah, problem is, you should've listened to me."

"True." Mark shrugged. "At least I was smart enough to move on before the bitch tried to neuter me."

"Yeah, then what would Emma have left? God knows without your balls, you'd be useless."

"Funny." Mark mock laughed. "C'mon, let's get you hitched."

Mark patted Matt's shoulder hard enough to nudge him forward. Matt checked his suit one last time in the floor-length mirror hanging on the back of the bedroom door. The mossy-green dress shirt he'd chosen looked great with his gunmetal-gray suit and tie. It even matched his dark brown hair and hazel eyes nicely and really brought out the bronze tone of his skin. He looked pretty great. Though, Luke probably looked ten times better.

"You want this flower thing?" his brother asked, pinching the stem of the calla lily boutonniere between his thumb and forefinger.

"Yeah," Matt said. "Can you pin it on my jacket?"

"Emma!" Mark yelled, and Matt flinched. The door cracked open, and Emma's very pregnant stomach appeared first. "Can you help him? I don't know how this thing works."

Emma laughed and shook her head. She waddled into the room and closed the door behind her. Mark handed the flower over to her, and she held it up to the lapel of Matt's suit. She had a contented smile on her radiant face and a motherly glow about her.

"You two make such a handsome couple," she said. Matt's heart thudded in his chest.

"Have you seen him? Is he ready? Does he look okay? Is he nervous?"

Emma laughed softly. "He is ready and yes, he's as nervous as you are. He's afraid you're going to chicken out at the last minute."

"Never."

"I know. That's what I told him. He won't be happy until he sees you joining him at the altar."

"The feeling is mutual," Matt said softly.

After Emma pinned the boutonniere to his lapel, she ran her dainty hand down the front of his suit jacket, then straightened his tie. "I think you're ready, Mr. Murphy." She gave him a smile, and he returned it, then kissed her forehead gently. As far as Matt was concerned, Mark had done damn good with Emma. She was a hell of a lot better for him than Constance had ever been.

"C'mon, little brother." Mark nodded. "Let's get this show on the road."

They walked down the stairs together—Mark beside Matt, Emma and Scotty behind them. The closer Matt came to walking down that aisle, the harder his heart pounded and the more his brow sweat. It wasn't for thinking he'd made a mistake. Nothing could've been further from the truth. It was very simply, a part of him feared Luke wouldn't be at the altar, that Luke would decide he'd made a mistake and really didn't want to spend the rest of his life with Matt. If something like that happened....

The doors opened, and the sound of violins playing pulled him away from his panic. He recognized the chords of the Lifehouse song Luke had chosen for them to walk up to the altar to. Matt took the first step, down onto the patio. It was a shaky step, and Matt had to close his eyes and take a few calming breaths before he dared to keep going. A few more steps, and his black dress shoe hit the edge of the white aisle runner.

C'mon, guy, pull yourself together. He'll be there. He loves you. Everything will be perfect. You'll see.

With one last exhale, Matt raised his chin and squared his shoulders. He glanced back. His brother stood directly behind him. Mark gave him a curt nod, and Matt started down the aisle.

Some of Luke's firefighter buddies had made the trip from Tennessee just for the occasion. Rows of their family and friends, people they hadn't seen in years, stood smiling. A few even had tears in their eyes. Matt couldn't look at them, or he knew he'd tear up too. After all, his hopes and dreams for his life culminated in this moment, with him walking down the aisle to join the man he loved more than anything in matrimony.

The violins sang out the next phrase of the song, and that's when he finally saw Luke appear from behind the trees, and Luke looked like heaven to him. He had a smile so wide it dimpled his cheeks. The sun made his blond hair radiant and made his blue eyes sparkle, or maybe that was the unbridled happiness twinkling in his stare. Whatever it was, it made Matt's heart beat faster, then slow to its normal pace. It took Matt's breath away. They met each other at the altar, and Matt immediately took Luke's hand.

The moment their palms touched and Luke's fingers intertwined with his, everything calmed—his racing pulse, ragged breaths, and trembling hands. Everything in the world suddenly felt so incredibly right, so undeniably perfect.

"Family and friends," the officiant said. "We're gathered here today to join Matthew Jacob Murphy and Lukas Ryan Bishop in holy matrimony. If anyone wishes to protest, speak now or forever hold your peace."

Matt and Luke exchanged a glance, nervously waiting for that one asshole to spoil their perfect day, but no one stood up. No one spoke up. The officiant continued.

The words the judge spoke were a low hum compared to the thoughts floating around in Matt's head and the steady thumping of his heart. He absently stroked his thumb back and forth across Luke's knuckles. The man standing beside him had given him paradise, had shown him what it truly meant to be loved unconditionally, and for that, Matt would happily give him his heart and soul. After all, his heart and soul only felt complete once Luke had professed his love to Matt.

The judge cleared his throat and whispered, "Your vows."

Luke gave him a nervous grin. Half the people sitting behind them laughed softly.

Matt said a quiet "oh" before turning to Luke and taking his other hand. He inhaled softly, then began to speak.

"Luke, when I got the call you'd been hurt, I honestly thought that was the end. I thought I would never get to tell you how I really felt. I thought I'd lost my chance to show you how much you mean to me and how much I love you. When you opened your eyes and spoke your first words, I knew God had given me another chance to do the right thing by you, and I swear, I want to spend the rest of my life making up for the years we missed together. I want to spend the rest of my life showing you how much I love you."

His voice became hoarse the moment he saw Luke's eyes turn glassy. He felt the familiar burn in his own stare and could almost taste his tears on the back of his tongue, but Matt swallowed them down because he had to keep going. He had to tell Luke everything he'd spent three months trying to write down on the piece of paper he'd ended up forgetting upstairs in the bedroom.

"Luke, you gave me hope. You gave me trust, but most of all, you gave me love. I vow to always be honest with you, to trust you in return. I vow to be patient and loving, and I promise to do my best to make you the happiest man I can. I love you."

"I love you too," Luke whispered, and everyone in the rows began to clap.

The hardest part was done. He'd said everything he'd wanted to say and got through the vows without choking up… too badly.

The judge raised his hand only slightly, and the crowd quieted. Luke said his vows, which weren't too much different from Matt's, even though they hadn't shared the first word with each other until that moment. Their hearts and minds, their bodies and souls were simply in the same place, on the same page, and it seemed as though they always would be, simply because they always had been. It just took a little over twenty years for them both to realize it.

Now, they wouldn't forget it.

They slid their matching titanium rings onto each other's fingers, keeping their stares locked. Then the officiant said, "By the authority vested in me by the state of Connecticut, it is my privilege to stand here on this seventeenth day of April, in the year two thousand and sixteen, and pronounce you as husbands. You may now kiss your groom."

The moment their lips met, everyone stood and cheered. Cameras flashed and clicked around them. Then everything faded into a backdrop as they met each other in the most meaningful kiss their lips had ever and would ever know. They were now joined, in matrimony, in front of all their friends and in the eyes of God and the state of Connecticut.

ALLISON CASSATTA was born and raised in Memphis, Tennessee, where she lives happily with her amazing husband of over a decade. She has written more than twenty books with gay, lesbian, bisexual, and heterosexual pairings. Her passion is the beauty of love and the art of words.

Allison's accolades include 2013 Top Pick of the Year from The Novel Approach, 2013 All Romance Ebooks Bestseller, 2012 Rainbow Book Awards Honorable Mention Winner, 2011 Best-selling Author, and 2011 Best Anthology. She is currently published with Dreamspinner Press, Fireborn Publishing, Amber Quill Press, and MLR Press.

Website: www.allisoncassatta.com
Twitter: @allisoncassatta
Facebook: www.facebook.com/allison.cassatta.page
Blog: allisoncassatta.blogspot.com
E-mail: info@allisoncassatta.com

DREAM 'TIL
MONDAY

ALLISON CASSATTA

When Hollywood comes a-knockin', a young, small-town Mississippi photographer named Sawyer Taylor packs his bags and heads to the West Coast. He's been hired to photograph for a romantic comedy in San Francisco and looks at the opportunity as a chance to rebuild and reclaim his life. But a quick, drunken hand job behind a bar in the Castro might prove a horrible mistake.

Film director Miles Eisenberg isn't a man who wants to commit. He has a daughter who means the world to him at home, and he worries over how his decisions might affect her. He comes up with a million good reasons not to give Sawyer a second look, but sometimes the heart is determined to love, and the brain can't convince it otherwise. His affair with Sawyer becomes a whirlwind romance worthy of the silver screen, but life doesn't always imitate art, and imperfect heroes don't always get their happy endings.

www.dreamspinnerpress.com

PATIENT PRIVILEGE

ALLISON CASSATTA

Dr. Erik Daniels knows how it feels to lose everything. His addiction to alcohol cost him his fiancé and his private practice, but he finally managed to regain control over his life and become a successful substance abuse counselor. He helps people regardless of their ability to pay. It isn't the dream life he had in San Francisco, but at least he has something to be proud of. Everything seems to be getting back on the right track until he meets Angel, a heroin-addicted male prostitute.

Erik not only sees a lot of himself in Angel but a great deal of potential as well. He's willing to sacrifice a lot to get Angel on the right path—but it will come at a cost to his carefully rebuilt career.

www.dreamspinnerpress.com

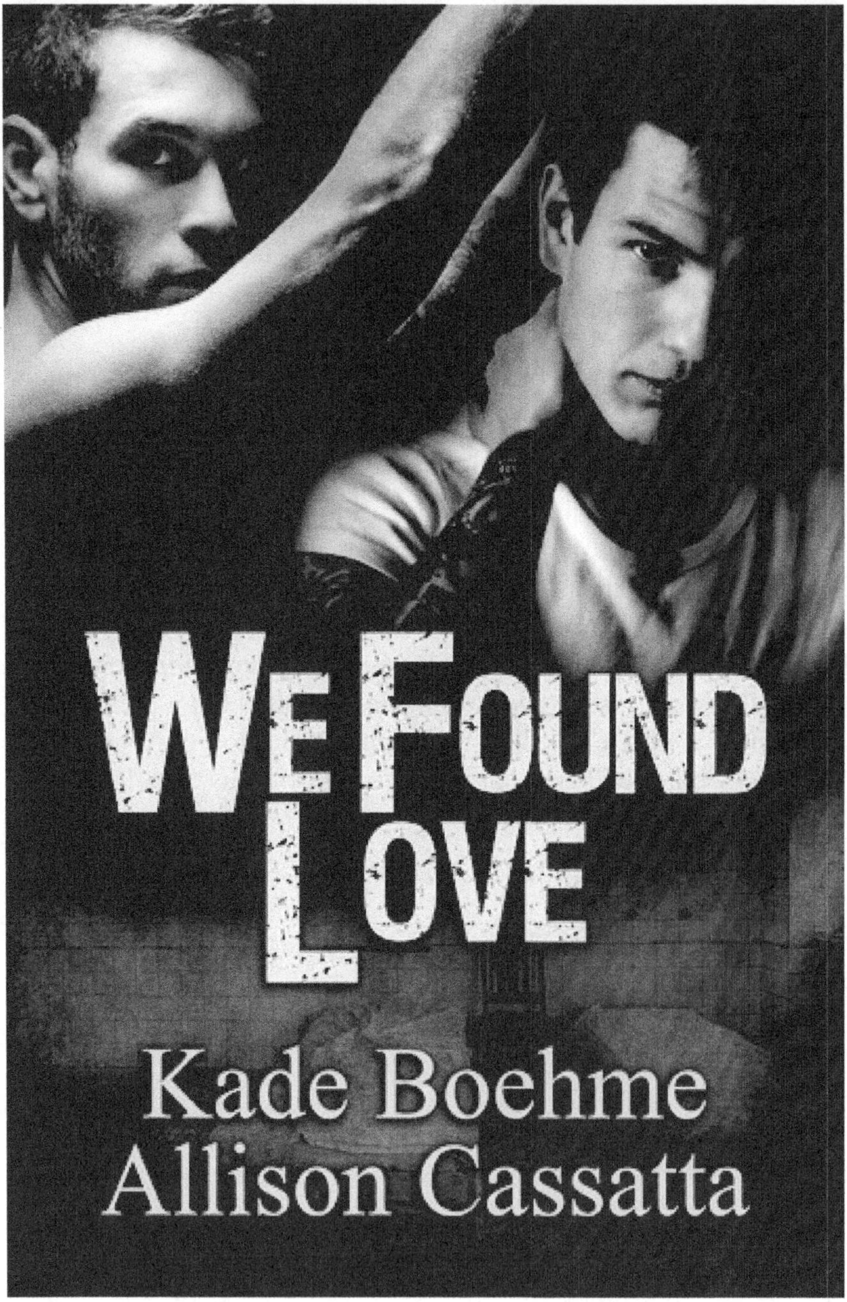
WE FOUND
LOVE
Kade Boehme
Allison Cassatta

It's no surprise Riley Connors is dealing with issues. He was kidnapped as a young boy, and his parents abandoned him after his newsworthy return. He bounced from foster home to facility and back. Now an adult, ghosts from his past continue to haunt him. After a suicide attempt, he is locked away in Hartfield so that people can make him tune in to emotions he has tried to bury.

Hunter Morgan had the kind of love that spans ages. But the stress of college and adulthood became too much to handle, and the love of Hunter's life turned to drugs. After he overdoses, Hunter finds himself soaring out of control on the same miserable path. His brother finds him and calls an ambulance, and the sister Hunter would rather not have calls it a suicide attempt, landing Hunter in Hartfield.

Finding love isn't easy, but it can happen under the most dire circumstances. Together Hunter and Riley may be able to grow from their pain. But they will need to learn to live for themselves, letting love come second.

www.dreamspinnerpress.com